CHAPTER ONE:

As the sun beamed through th............ing his skin, Mike woke. Taking a deep breath followed by a huge moan of tiredness he rose from his bed and stretched. He checked the clock on the wall, 3:47 am read the digital clock.

'fuck it, I'm up.'

He shot out of the bed and headed towards the bathroom, he'd been awake no longer than two minutes and it was already on his mind

'The 5th' he whispered as he tried not to urinate on the seat.

Four bodies had been found in the space of 3 months due to Mike's actions, his need to feel the light's 'go out as he called it had cost four innocent women their lives. Everything they were, everything they could have been was all gone. It never crossed his mind he was erasing their future as well as their existence, who knows one of the four women could have cured cancer and he could have robbed the world of that privilege. He checked his face in his small wall mirror, he was searching for the bags all the sleepless nights should have given him, but he was clear. The call for killing had always been inside of him from such a young age but since he's been acting on it, he can't get a wink. The only time he sleeps well is when he's snapped a finger.

He started the electric shower and stepped inside. A red-hot shower is how Mike always started his day, the numbness of his existence could never feel the temperature he ran the shower at, but the steam and mold on the small apartment's ceiling suggested otherwise. Within an hour Mike was dressed and ready for work, his job at the council as a bin man wasn't too demanding and it suited his life as well as his needs. He used their routes to select his victims or the 'SHIT' as he called them. His second victim used to work in the offices of the council, around 6 weeks ago Mike bumped into the attractive young women in the break room at work, they both were making a coffee, they got talking about their job and home life, mike lying through his teeth as usual. As soon as he saw the ring, he knew he wanted her, he wanted to feel her lights go out. He wanted to show her how he felt about the whole sanctity of marriage. On his route the day after he was talking to Ben and Troy about her, saying how he'd like to 'fuck her brains out' Ben and Troy were common guys, Barnsley born and bred as they say, well known in the town as the town's clowns because they had been friends for years and had a funny story about pretty much anything. They agreed with Mike and on their round, they showed Mike where she lived in case he ever plucked up the courage to make a move. Troy had once walked her home after she had fallen in the street, drunk. By that night on the 2nd of February at 7:08 pm, she had her finger snapped. He had strangled her like he wanted to in the break room, he strangled her with that much force her eyes looked like they had popped out of her skull. He simply knocked on her door claiming to have broken down, playing dumb. She offered him to use her phone, she only met him once and he had gained her complete trust. They shared a laugh about their encounter in the break room, he scanned the house for noise of anyone else been there. If her husband was at home, it would have saved her life. Silence was his queue to proceed.

Mike didn't start work until six. As he searched the cupboards for a box of coco pops, the dog was scratching his water bowl. Mike hated people but he loved dogs. Dogs never betrayed you or let you down they simply loved and showed nothing but kindness. Marley was a black and white Springer Spaniel with the bubbly personality to match Mike's madness. As mike looked down at his beloved pet, he couldn't help but feel his past. He remembered how he used to be like that, all-loving and kind. That was before the truth was revealed to him about people. Mike made his way to the sofa to sit down and eat his cereal. He checked the clock to see it was only 4:17 am. He rested his eyes and began to dream. Dreams of his torture and pain.

When Mike was nine years of age that's when it was at its worst. He lived in the same town he always loved. Barnsley wasn't for the faint-hearted. Full of drug users and scumbags. The type of people that would rob their grandmother for a hit. It wasn't anything special but to Mike, it was home. There wasn't much to do in the town it was a very plain place to live, if you weren't addicted to drugs or into stealing valuables then you'd have a very dull day. His Father Dave Ashburn had a small Butchers shop in the town, He was famous for his home-made pork pies and for being a very kind generous man. He did a lot for charity and did his bit for the homeless by handing out his unsold pork pies at 4 pm every day. His mother Sally Ashburn was the complete opposite.

Her wicked ways always came to light when his dad or Mike did anything wrong, or right for that matter. The main thing Mike remembers from his childhood was his punishment's his witch of a mother gave him. The small cupboard under the stairs is where he spent most of his time for been late or cheeky, but mainly because his mother felt like putting him in there. He used to beg not to be put in the 'scary cupboard' but he ended up in there against his will most of the time. Mike always begged his father to get his mum tested for a mental illness of some kind, but David was too scared, he didn't dare to cross her, not after the last time. One day David said he would be home for dinner, but he was an hour late. In a blind rage, Sally slammed Mike into the wall then into his cupboard. He stayed in there for about three hours, when she let him out, he found his father with a snapped finger. His dads' wedding finger had been back so far it snapped like a twig. On the last night of their marriage, She stayed up waiting for him to get home from the pub, he'd been out with work colleagues and treated his staff to free drinks. David and Sally had been fighting for months about anything and everything but mainly his snapped finger, the doctor said it wouldn't ever serve its full function again. When he came home, Sally found lipstick on his collar, that's when his mother snapped. Mike knew it was because his mum never loosened her grip, constantly smothering him. That night Mike woke up to find his mum out on the landing looking into his room. He could hear her talking to herself.

'mum? Are you ok?' the question was answered by footsteps rushing towards him, as he laid there a terrified nine-year-old, his mother hovered over him.

'I... I smother him?' her soft voice whispered.

Her pale blue eyes turned to pure tears and anger.

'I'll show him smothering! Get up!' before Mike could say a word, he was getting dragged by his pajama sleeve. As she rushed him down the stairs only one thing came into his mind.

The dreaded chamber. The chamber was dark and full of rot, but at least while he was in there out of the way he was safe. He knew he'd be in there all night while his mother screamed and threw plates and whatever else was in her reach at his beloved father. As the pale white cupboard door slammed shut locking him in for the night, Mike woke up.

5:12 am, Mike rubbed his eyes and stroked the short bristles on his face. He swept his brown hair back into formation where it belonged. His fringe swept out of the way of his eyesight. He stood up and opened the patio door for Marley.

'I know Marls, she was a bitch'

After a few minutes, he kissed his dog on the top of his head as he re-entered the apartment and Mike closed the sliding door.

'Be a good boy while I'm gone, I won't be long buddy.' He walked to his apartment door, swinging it open with some force, so it woke his neighbour, and headed to his round.

CHAPTER TWO:

As the cold air blew against his face, Mike wished he was back at his place. His small crummy apartment with his furry best friend was the second thing on his mind. The first was the nagging of the 5th. Mike enjoyed hunting and finding new victims. until he killed his first, Mike would get intense migraines that could give him earache. His head used to feel a mile wide until he snapped and turned out her lights. His first victim was a tall blonde woman. She was married for 7 years happily. Mike got chatting to her in a bar in the town. The Swivel bar was notorious for drug use and fights. People go in for the sole purpose of destroying brain cells and breaking jaws. The entrance to the bar was located on the south side of peel parade. Just opposite the beer garden to Weatherspoon's, there stood the swivel bar, in all its shit stained glory. The bottom floor of the bar hosted a clerk you payed to enter, a roid munching door man to kick you back into the street if you tried anything clever. And a restroom usually covered in vomit and cheap cocaine. On the night they met Mike convinced her he was a good guy, a rich guy who was in the town for business. She liked what she saw, he scrubbed up well.

'What do you say? Shall we take this back to my place?' she asked with a hint of lust in her voice. Before she could grab her coat, they were out the door and making their way to the taxi rank. Mike thought it too good to be true. A married woman taking him home to rock his world, he thought it was his dad looking down on him, but he knew that wasn't true.

They arrived at her house in Royston. Her three bedroomed house stood proud. The garden welcomed them with open arms, almost saying this is a family house and we welcome you. As Mike entered and observed the beautiful sight of family photos and decretive flowers his migraines flared up like a fire work. As he tried to observe her sculptured ass, he couldn't help but close his eyes in agonising pain.

'Have you got and painkillers please? My head is a fucking shed.' He said in agony

'Yeah, sure one sec would you like a coffee or anything?' She replied blushing as she noticed him itching his crotch.

'Yes, please babe' Mike said in relief.

She hurried into the kitchen to make her stud a brew. Mike couldn't see with the tears in his eyes. He stumbled into her living room only to fall on to her freshly cleaned carpet. He turned over to face the ceiling. He always wondered why he got migraines at moments when it mattered. The migraines started when he turned 16 years old. Still in his mother's care which never helped with any part of his life. He blamed her for everything that was wrong him and rightly so. As his head grew in pain, his ears started to ring. Forcing his temples to spasm.

'You always were a problem.'

'What? Who said that?' Mike asked in panic. He recognised that voice. He's heard that voice all his life but, in the hallucination, it was muffled to start with. As his mother's voice grew in tone his head started to burn.

'Your father would be so disappointed'

'Shut up, shut up SHUT UP! don't you dare talk about him!'

He held his head, tight. Trying to counter the pressure of the migraine.

Mike's new friend entered the living room, bringing him his brew and painkillers.

'Hey, who are you-'

Before she could finish her question, Mike pounced on her knocking her to the ground. On her way down she hit her head on the coffee table busting he skull open at that back like a balloon.

Mike took hold of her neck as hard he could until the manifestation of the witch left him as well as his migraine. She kept gasping for air and trying to grab anything for a weapon. Mike was screaming in her face, telling her to leave him alone. As her eyes turned red from the blood vessels bursting in the whites of her eye, he saw her true face. It was over, this innocent woman was a mother, a wife and now she Mike's first. As he released his grip from her pale neck, he caught a glimpse of her wedding ring.

'A married woman willing to cheat on her husband. Fucking piece of shit'

He walked over to her hand, put his hands in his sleeve to cover his prints. Placed the wedding finger in his hand and snapped it like a twig. Then wiped her neck with her blood from her left eye to wash away his prints on her neck. He stood up straight and felt his migraine lift away like the sun after the storm. He took one last look at her cold dead eyes and, indulging the horror of what he just did. Mike wasn't upset or even shaken for that matter, he was.... uplifted.

Mike used his shirt to wipe away anymore prints he may have left. The coffee cup after he drank it, the family photo he looked at on his way in. No evidence he was ever there.

Every morning while he waited for his lift, he thought of that cheating woman. He often complimented the memory with a cheap cigarette. Inhaling the delicious poison into his lungs. Each draw making him more awake. Around five minutes passed, he finally heard his lift screeching around the corner. Ben and Troy often drove like mad men in the early hours, Mike could never tell who was behind the wheel until he got into the cab. With a loud squeak the truck came to holt.

'Morning gorgeous'

That was the usual greeting of the pair. This time it came from Troy, Ben was driving. Troy was a usual looking guy, short brown hair, eyes to match, lean build. Mike often thought if he was to kill him it would be easy to move his body, his cocky attitude often made him grind his teeth, but he'd never killed a man before, he didn't see the point or feel the need to. After all it was his mother he hated, he loved his dad to the ends of the earth.

'Jump in Mike, we got to make a start kid.' Uttered Ben.

Ben was Mikes favourite of the two. His giant beer belly and his stupidly formed moustache made Mike laugh inside his mind, he'd laugh himself sick when he'd finish the round. He didn't hate him or even dislike him, his look was just comical. Without the moustache he'd look like a normal man. His casual face expressions expressed his wisdom of the world and that he was full of advice and life lessons. Mike would take his advice on cooking and money saving tips but never about facial hair. Mike jumped in the cab, pushing Troy into the middle seat and into Ben's personal space. 'Fuck! Were late guys, we've got a meeting at ten past six. Fuck sake Troy!' said ben in a panic.

'What? I was on time, I always am, it's your shit ability to drive this bag shit.' Replied Troy

Mike sparked up a secondary smoke as Ben put the gas pedal to floor.

CHAPTER THREE:

As they arrived in the yard of the council's depot, the rain started to hammer the windscreen. Coming down like daggers from the sky, as if sending a warning. Mike always enjoyed the rain, he enjoyed the coldness of the purest water. The way it would wash over him, he couldn't help but feel safe. He felt protected. The main building stood at the back of the yard. The windows emerged in darkness sending a 'back off' vibe and not to be entered. The pale white rendered walls twinkled like snowflakes in the wind. The three-story building was one of the places Mike loved visiting. He mainly enjoyed the break room, where he met the second. He stared up at the window of the room, his eyes snapped shut sending him back in time to her house. Her swollen neck, her corpse, her finger snapped. He loved them all. Ben exited the truck and dangled one leg in the air. He landed with a big thud on the wet concrete followed by his laces splashing in the puddle. Troy followed and slid out the driver's seat with ease, his lean build made him like a whippet. He was agile and cocky. Never a good mix Mike thought. The three of them raced inside to get out of the tidal wave which was sweeping South Yorkshire. The wettest winter on record was sending the north and most of the east into panic. Places were flooding within minutes of the rainfall. Most news stations had reports of people missing and people dead in their own homes. Mainly the elderly. The scum of the town was taking advantage of the flash floods to get what they needed from the vulnerable. They took possessions, clothes, food. Anything that could get them quick cash to pay for their bad habits. Mike often got angered about this. He thought about taking out the scum before, but he knew he couldn't kill them all. He didn't even understand his urges. He had spoken to women since his first victim and they lived to see the light of day. He didn't have control like he wanted. He would feel it from afar, edging closer and closer until it was so close it would appear as a witch. His mother would get inside his head and pull his strings. She'd pull so hard he could feel his head about to explode until unleashed his rage. He didn't care who suffered for it, as long she was gone that's all he cared for. She'd not appear for days but even Mike knew she wasn't taking her time anymore. She was getting more frequent and the fear of seeing the inside of a jail cell, with her to taunt him was too much. He knew he had to be careful, to be mindful of his actions and his victims, but he knew the urge to kill wasn't going away anytime soon.

As they entered the building, most of the staff were still sat in their cars. They rushed upstairs to the meeting room. They were greeted by a table full of suited big shots. They all looked identical, one after another dressed in pin-striped suits and brown shoes. The odd one had a beard like Mike's, bristles and a sad look on the face.

'You're late' said a firm voice. The man stood with a dominate presence and a dirty stare aimed at the three of them. 'This is a warning, at 3 PM we need you back here for questioning.'

'Questioning about what?' asked Ben with a confused look on his face.

'Questions about Lauren, look none of you are in any sort of trouble'

'Who's Lauren?" asked Mike with a sense that he didn't care.

"Lauren is the women who was found stone dead with her finger snapped...that monster"

Mike's heart dropped when he realised who they were talking about, he did his absolute best not to look nervous, but he knew he looked out of place as soon as he heard the truth. I could do with some rain right now he thought.

'None of you are suspects, it's just some questions.' Uttered the man in a stern tone of voice, as if to say man up.

'Sure, what time shall we be back for?' said Troy in a cheery tone not realising that he had this information.

'Be back for no later than 3 pm'

'You got it, come on lads we've got bins to empty' said Troy as he turned around signaling the rest of his crew to follow his lead.

Mike and Ben followed him out of the office and down the hall.

'Didn't know you cared so much about her Troy, you seemed very quick to help the crows' laughed Ben. The crows had been their name for years now, ever since Ben said they started to shit on the people below them and constantly peck at them, pecking away and shitting on them none stop.

'Well you know I fucking hate their guts Ben, but Lauren was a lovely woman. She always smiled at me, in fact I can't remember her face without a smile plastered on it." Said Troy in a soft voice, Remembering the time he had walked her home.

Troy couldn't but Mike could. He knew what she looked like with the life drained out her, without the lights on. The more he thought about the closer he could feel the wave of rage growing closer. He knew soon he would face the wicked witch of his past.

'Do you remember her mike?' asked Ben

Mike glanced at him as he thought about his response. 'Yeah a little did she have red hair?' he already knew the answer to that. He knew a lot more things about her than Troy and Ben ever will. He knew she took her shoes off in the house. He knew she wore a thong, he remembered the red lace between her ass cheeks as she walked through her hallway. The leggings she was wearing the night her lights went out were almost see-through and he also knew what she sounded like gasping for oxygen. The way she would say please with a tight hand wrapped around her throat always echoed in Mike's mind. Whenever he shut his eyes at night, he could hear them all, begging.

"Yeah, she was a bird I'll tell thi." Troy's Barnsley accent let out.

'She was okay' replied mike. 'Anyway lads, we better make a move'

The three of them walked down the last flight of stairs, across the hallway and into the daggers of the rain.

CHAPTER FOUR:

Smithies lane was the last stop on Mike's route and home to a decent amount of people. The long crumbling roads always kicked up a fuss in the town's council meetings. There was never enough funding for the town. Traffic lights, public parks and the roads where the three main things that suffered neglect, but the list went on and on. Loraine Watson was having none of it though, she had had enough. When she was 7 years old, her father was sent to prison for twenty-four months due to tax evasion. Loraine and everyone in town knew that her father was innocent of the accusations. They all knew it was because he came close to been the next elected mayor of Barnsley. Crushing the current mayor Joseph King in polls. Loraine made it her life's mission to expose the corruption of the failing council and fix the major problems not just affecting her but the whole community, but most of all, for her children. Her son Jake was riding his bike down the lane and hit a pothole. Sending him flying like Evil Kinevil. Breaking part of his neck. He made a full recovery, but he spent many months in hospital and regaining the function of his neck muscles. Loraine had been married for 7 years to her husband James. They had a beautiful two-bedroom house on smithies lane. The house stood facing north, surrounded by trees. The house was originally a bungalow but before their wedding, they expanded. Their son Jake was five years old with autism. It put stress on their happily ever after, but they survived, they always did. James was grateful for his beautiful wife, standing proud at 5"6 her hair always blew in the wind with such grace and secrets. It's the one thing James fell in love with when they first met. On that night in the swivel bar. He saw her long blonde hair bouncing to the beat on the dancefloor. The rest was history.

They ventured through the countries together, they explored each other's bodies in passion and lust. They eventually moved in together and decided to settle down. Jake came unexpectedly but it humbled them, and the doting new parents knew what they wanted to do with their lives. Loraine always wanted to be a mother even though it took a toll on her fantastic figure and her perky assets, she found it necessary to achieve her long-life goal. Motherhood would welcome her with unforgiving arms. Smithies lane had a history of unforgiving mothers and with the snapper lurking in the town, who knew if it could gain another.

CHAPTER 5:

Mike took his last draw on his cheap cigarette before exiting the vehicle. His size ten boots landed on the hard tarmac as he flicked his tab end into the drain. He looked at the street sign. Smithies lane was where he had tried his first ever smoke. To him, it was always a special street to share such a precious memory. Ben and Troy exited the cab to the pouring rain, putting their hoods up of their waterproofs. Gazing at all the rubbish bins piled up on the street. Standing at the end of each house like a knight standing guard.

'Let's get to work boys' Said Troy in an upbeat tone. Mike wasn't in the mood for lifting bins, he could feel the storm getting closer. He knew soon it would be here to greet him. He decided it was time to pick a new piece of shit to kill. Just the thought of turning out someone's lights put him in the mood to 'shift some bins' and just like that the hunt was on. One after the other the bins were flying on and off the truck. Mike was in the zone. Scanning every property, he went near for the sign of a loving home one with a wife and husband. 'Jesus! have you smoked you're Weetabix this morning kid?' asked Ben.

'Ha, no man I just want to get it over and done with, plus we have to be back by half two remember?' replied Mike.

'Oh, shit yeah, Troy get your head out of your ass and pick up the pace.'

Troy hated it when Mike was in this mood, Mike's need to kill always made him suffer a hard day's work, and he never knew why.

As Mike approached the nicest house he had ever seen, he felt his senses kick up a gear. The tall white house was surrounded by a sense of freedom and the driveway was at least 12 metres in length. As Mike walked down the long straight path, he started to take note of every detail. He knew this would be the perfect place for a wife to live her life in. It's perfect in every way. Plenty of space inside the property, he could tell by looking at the size of the windows. Perfectly stacked like a house of cards.

Wow must have some money behind them he thought. He could tell more than two people were living there. No woman would ever hang a picture of dogs playing poker in the living room. The white wallpaper made it impossible to miss. He also noticed the flowers on the landing window, no man would have flowers. The flowers were a bunch of fake roses that gave a beautiful personality to the upper floor of the house. Loraine mainly stuck to the upstairs out of her husband's way. He had a habit of neglecting her needs. Football and PlayStation came before her or his beautiful blessing. The downstairs was a beautiful layout for any family. The living room housed a giant three-seater sofa, perfect for match days on Sky Sports. The cream carpet was spotless. Like it had been cleaned by professionals every week. The beautiful oak dining table sat cheerfully in between the living room and the kitchen. Dividing the loving couple, the table was a mutual meeting ground for their crumbling marriage. Mike started to drift away from the bin towards the house, getting side-tracked by the thought of a wife being home. He decided to look behind the property in the garden and to search for any cameras. Trying to take a little care with this one. If he was going to kill her, he had to make sure he wasn't going to get caught. With the four other victims, they all had small houses, nothing on the scale to this monstrosity. There were two cars parked out front, one black land rover sport and one pink mini cooper countryman. No man would drive one of those by choice thought Mike. He walked down the narrow path to the garden. Tiptoeing his way over the flags and loose stones trying not to draw attention. He peered around the corner to find a beautifully laid green lawn. A child's climbing frame and swing set and a giant oak tree. Aging at least 100 years old. Mike was stunned by the image which sat in front of him. The garden told a story of family life. He could see a child been pushed on his swing and then maybe a game of hide and seek using the oak tree as the base point. Something which Mike dreamed of when he was a kid. A loving family was the one thing he would never possess. If his dad would have made it through that night things could have been different for all of them, but his childhood was spent in the dreaded chamber.

'Excuse me? Can I help you?'

Mike turned around in a flash to see who dare interrupt his train of thought. There she was, number five. Her long blonde hair sat perfectly on her shoulders drawing his attention to her perky rack. Mike examined her up and down. Her pale blue eyes stared at him in a fury, warning him to leave. Mike clapped his eyes on what he was looking for. Her shiny gold wedding ring twinkled as the rain droplets trickled down the diamond.

'Oh, hello, yes I can't seem to find your bin. I thought I'd check in case you forgot to leave it out.'

He gazed at her hoping she bought his lame story.

'It's out front, I put it there myself, you blind or something?' her voice was like an out of tune Ukulele to Mike's ears.

'Sorry ma'am I couldn't see it, sorry.' Mike turned around and began to smile with excitement

'Fucking council, useless.' Her hatred of the council wasn't undetected.

Mike walked back down the path with joy in his steps, as the storm grew nearer so did the 5th. Mike knew she was it, as soon as he looked in her pale blue eyes, he felt the sparks fly inside him. She was the one he was going to kill. He double-checked the path for any cameras, there was none. He didn't see any in the garden and there were none out front. 'Shame it could have saved your life' he thought.

As he grabbed her bin, he noticed an old woman staring at him. Her purple coat was drenched from the downpour. Her small Jack Russell was shaking dying to go indoors but she just stared at him.

'You okay love?' Asked Mike as he waited for any sign of life from her, she was as still as a statue.

'Ah yes, just lost myself there darling, have a good one my love' her voice screeched from the street.

Mike turned and faced the truck which was still stationary.

'Come on Mike we haven't got all fucking day.' Shouted Ben while he sat in his cab.

'Coming lads.' He replied. Ben was right they didn't have all day, and neither did the women at 22 smithies lane. Mike had decided within five minutes tonight was going to be the night 'The Snapper' as the press called him would claim his 5th victim. The thought of her beautiful body lying lifeless on her floor comforted Mike. He couldn't wait for her lights to go out. He had decided to show around 8 pm to scope the place out. He didn't know if she was going to be alone, but he didn't care he'd wait for his chance. Surely there would be an opportunity for him to get his release he was craving. And if not, he'd create one. If her husband was home, he would have to find a way to get him out of the house. And he had the perfect idea in mind. What's the only thing snobs care about other than their kids? Material items. He would have to get him out of the house so his car would be the target, assuming the douche bag drove that land rover. After he finishes his round, he would go to the meeting then a quick pit stop at the local B&Q for a can of red spray paint. Mike had never done anything like this before, his plan was simple, spray his car, get him to chase him and lose him in the woods. Being a big shot, he knew image was a big thing, so he'd be wanting to get it sorted straight away. He hoped. Mike jumped back in the cab and they headed to the next street over to finish their route. See you later beautiful he thought as the truck roared around the corner.

CHAPTER SIX:

As the rain finally came to a holt, the truck entered the yard. The time was 2:26 PM. The gang had just made it with time to spare, they had a rep of never being on time, so this was a rare occasion. A herd of police cars covered the entrance to the building. Three cops stood outside having a smoke. 'I could do with a smoke' uttered Mike, the lack of nicotine was making him on edge. He could feel the storm approaching.

'No time!' said Troy. They all rushed inside, hoping not to disappoint the bosses yet again. They hadn't fully forgiven Ben for crashing one of the old trucks. They all ran up the steep flight of stairs to reach the 2nd floor. As they turned the corner after the lifts, they were greeted by the snob in the suit. His eyes said that he was in no mood for games. 'Sit there and wait to be called' he said in a stern voice. The three of them sat there twiddling their thumbs. Mike couldn't help noticing the police officers in the financial office. All the draws had been flung open in a search to any kind of lead as to what happened to the poor girl. Little did they know the culprit was sitting less than 4ft away. Mike accidentally made eye contact with a standing officer. His tall presence made him feel uneasy. His deep brown eyes pierced Mike like a sword. He knows he thought in panic. Automatically thinking the worse he sat as still and tried to become invisible to his wandering eyes.

'Sir, come and have a look at this.' The tall officer left his post to see what his colleague had found.

Thank god, that must be one of my worst nightmares he thought in relief. The brief encounter made Mike realise he must not get caught. He came up with a plan to answer every question they threw at him as honest as he could. Not to give any signs he was lying. The last thing he wanted was to be a name on their books.

'Mike Ashburn?'

The call of his name came from his left, he looked around, but the figure was gone. The door swung slightly on the old hinges as Mike approached the bright red door. As he stepped inside the room two police officers shadowed either side of the doorway. Their tall posture gave a controlling vibe to the small room. In front of all the office file boxes sat a man at an old chipped desk. He stood up and stuck out his muscular arm.

'Mike, I'm detective Jack Brown for the South Yorkshire police. Please have a seat.'

Mike sat down on the office swivel chair. He took a big gulp and said hello back in the calmest voice he could find.

'You are not in any kind of trouble Mike, I'm questioning everyone about your colleague Lauren. But you must understand that everything we say can't leave this room, cool?'

His arms were open waiting for Mike to respond. His combed back hair matched his brown shoes to the shade. His face was full of bags and creases which suggested he'd been up all night long. His red buttoned shirt was hanging a black-tie loosely around his neck and his black trousers had matching cufflinks.

'Cool' he replied.

'Ok Mike, how well did you know Lauren?' asked Jack.

'Not very well to be fair, I only met her once in the break room and that was about a week ago.' He answered honestly. So good so far.

'Ok, what did you guys talk about? 'Asked the detective caressing his short stubble.

'Not much to be fair, we were both making a brew and we got talking about coffee. And then a little about our jobs.' He said with a little twist of the truth. He thought it best to leave out the bit where she told him her address.

'Ok, I see. What did you think about Lauren as a person?'

'What do you mean?' he asked puzzled.

'Like, do you think she had any enemy's, do you have any idea who would have wanted her dead?' The question rolled off his tongue with ease. Jack asked questions like these a lot.

"We all have enemy's detective, but I don't know anyone who associated with her.' He replied. But I do know someone who wanted her dead, me. It was me you, stupid fuck, He thought. The fact Laurens killer was sat directly opposite the man who was trying to catch him made him giggle under his breathe.

'Yeah, true. I have many as you can imagine. Did you notice anything on the day she died? Like did she act different in any way, any way at all?' the detective sat waiting for Mike's reply.

Mike saw the golden opportunity to send Jack on a wild goose chase. Just a false bit of information would keep him occupied and away from Mike. Well until tonight when he kills Loraine.

'Now that you mention it, she was acting a bit off' said Mike with a blank look on his face. Trying his best not to give any tell signs he was lying.

'I did notice that she did go for smoke at the back of building about 2 PM, and she was on the phone to someone. I think she was arguing because she was talking with her hands if you know what I mean.' He glanced at the detective to see his eyebrows were raised and scribbling in his pocketbook.

'But she didn't smoke Mike. I've checked with everyone and no one has ever seen her take a single drag.' He leaned back in the chair to express he wasn't convinced.

'I know, that's why it's odd right?' asked Mike almost letting slip that it was bullshit.

The detective leaned forward again placing his hairy arms in the triangle position on the desk.

'Hmm, yeah it is. Something must have stressed her out enough to make her do that, and you said she was on the phone? Any idea who to?'

He'd bought it Mike thought to his proud self.

'No, I saw her when I came back from my route. So I didn't hear anything' He said in a snap.

The brief interview came to a halt when Jack's phone rang.

'Yeah, I'll call you back.' He said and hung up the phone.

'It's the office so I think we'll leave it their MR Ashburn. If you think of any more information, please give me a call.' He handed Mike one his neatly printed white cards.

'I will do detective' Mike said in relief. He'd done it. He had been interviewed by the man who was hunting him and didn't arouse any suspicion from the police. Barnsley had no idea who the Snapper was and had zero leads. Mike was feeling invincible as he exited the room walking past the two officers standing guard. The only thing that could top his feeling off was with Loraine's lights going out. Jack's phone rang again. He answered with 'detective brown, speaking?'

It was his office and the sergeant and was on the other end.

'Anything Jack?' asked Sergeant Dickson. He had been on the force for many years and knew a lie from the truth, so Jack always shot straight with him.

'Nothing chief I'm afraid.' He said in an uneasy voice.

'I want this guy caught Jack! four body's in three months'! We need justice for those poor families.'

'I know sir, I promise you we'll get him, he's sloppy.' He said hoping to reassure the boss.

'Did you find anything in the office?'

'Again, come up empty. Although I have a report of the victim having a smoke and a very heated phone call on the day she died.' Jack said clearing his dry cough. He needed some rest desperately. He hadn't slept right in days. The pressure of four body's in three months with no leads was getting to him.

'So? What the hell does that have to do with her death, she died in her home!' Replied the annoyed voice on the phone. Jack could almost feel his spit come through the speaker when he spoke.

'I know that, but she didn't smoke. That phone call was enough to make her need some relief.' Said Jack as he started to smile, hoping the good news was enough.

'Find out who she was on the phone to and do it fast.' Before Jack could mumble the line went dead.

'Talk about gratitude' He uttered in an annoyed tone.

He exited the small file room to see two men sitting there unquestioned. Ben and Troy were next in line for the detective to interview. Mike had gone to feed his lungs.

'Wrap it guys were done.' Shouted Jack. 'It's okay boys, I have what I need' Lied the detective. He just wanted some sleep and he thought the phone call was going to lead him to the killer anyway. Ben and Troy had got up and went to meet Mike outside the building. Mike was stood smoking his precious cigarette with a great feeling. Like he had just won the lottery.

'Quitting time boys' Said Troy as he skipped to the truck.

They all got in the old beat-up rubbish truck with a sense of freedom. It was off to Troy's house first as he lived closer, then to Mike's. Ben came back to the depot to drop off the truck and then he went home. It was the driver's job to drop them off if they got called back to the office. They usually got dropped off as soon as they finished the route. Mike couldn't wait to get home and see Marley. He missed him like crazy when he went to work. The main reason he couldn't wait to get home was so the storm could be satisfied. Loraine's life was coming to an end and Mike couldn't take another minute without his hands wrapped around her neck.

CHAPTER SEVEN:

As Mike exited the cab, he stood on the pavement opposite his block of flats. He pulled a cigarette out and lit it. His first draw of the sweet nicotine filled smoke was like heaven on earth. It was just what he needed after the day he had. At least the main objective was complete. The fifth victim was selected. He couldn't wait to snap her finger. He crossed the road and headed to the main doors. The tower block was four stories high, supporting around 50 flats. He noticed his high visibility clothing was covered in dirt and odd-smelling goo. The juice from the bottom of the bins always found a way onto his work clothes. The smell was strong, so strong it always made him gip. Mike couldn't wait to get to his sacred space. His apartment was only small, but it homed one of his great loves. His Dog. Marley had been with him since he was a puppy. It was the only thing he truly loved in this cruel world. Mike saw an advert on the internet that he was for sale in Sheffield. He made the journey the day after to go and see him, just to see if he was ok but he ended up leaving with him. That morning Marley had been playing in the building sand they had in the garden. The ungrateful family was having a conservatory built and Marley took full advantage and got up to some mischief as he always did. Now he was older he was a lot calmer and more obedient, and more like a companion than a dog. Mike typed in the code for the door and entered. He headed straight to see his bud, he ran to his door and opened it. There to greet him was a very wagging tail attached to a panting spaniel. 'Hey, buddy! You miss me?' His question was answered by a loud bark. Luckily for Mike, the bottom flats of Stone Brooke house were made especially for pets. At the back of the flats stood a tall patio door which led to the yard for all the dogs. It had water bowls and a dog shit bin and plenty of concrete ground for them to enjoy the fresh air. He entered the flat and chucked his work bag by the door. He walked to the living area and collapsed on the sofa. Taking a moment to appreciate the worn-out leather, he let a great big gasp out. Letting all the negative vibes exit his body. His relaxing exhale was interrupted by the sound of Marley's nails scratching the glass of the patio door.

'Ok, buddy one sec.' He stood up and opened the patio for him. About five minutes passed and he scratched to come back in. He let him in and they both started to fuss each other on the sofa. They had both missed each other so much. Mike could always depend on him never to let him down in any way. Marley had never even made a mess in the flat. Mike headed to the bathroom and turned on the shower. He couldn't wait to get rid of the stench of foul bins. He planned to shower, get a bite to eat, walk his best buddy and then to take the fifth. As he got undressed, he noticed his migraine was flaring up again. His head started to pulsate in odd rhythm.

Coming then going but not in sync. He entered the shower to see the mold was still clinging to the tiles like a refugee to the bottom of a wagon. The warm water washed the stressful day away. His encounter with detective Jack Brown had put him on edge but it was easily fixed by his smoking habit. He washed himself from head to toe. Got to be clean head to toe when I'm going to such a fancy house he thought followed by a small chuckle. The hot water couldn't hide the fact the storm was fast approaching. His migraine had doubled in pain since it first started. His head was pounding, feeling like it would explode any minute. He didn't know if it was because of the storm or the lack of sleep since he had started killing. He turned the shower off and put pressure on his temples hoping for some relief.

'You always loved to be clean.' Mike shot around to see the shower door covered in condensation.

'What the...who said that?' the migraine had made his vision blurred. He could barely see the door which was less than a foot away from him. The migraine grew stronger and more intense, never leaving the front of his head. The pain felt like blades that had been heated up to match the earth's core. He could feel them trying to shoot through his skull. His ears started to ring as they got closer to the inside of his skin. He opened his eyes after squinting so hard he gave himself crow's feet. There was someone stood at the other side of the glass door.

'It's okay Michael, I'm here.' There was only one person who ever used his proper name. He knew as soon as she said it, and he could tell it was his mother by the sore sounding voice. With all his energy and focus, he tried to focus on the figure. Inching closer to the glass he could just make out the outline of her thin posture, he could see her shoulder-length hair flowing like she was stood on a hill in the wind. He wiped the glass in an aggressive motion banging on the glass as he did so. He opened his eyes as wide as he could to see the bathroom empty. She had gone but she was still there. He could still feel her hatred towards him lingering in the air, like a bad smell.

'I've got to get my shit together.' He said in a sickly voice. He rubbed his eyes as hard as he could. He grabbed his towel and exited the shower. He covered the floor with water droplets as he walked into his bedroom. He quickly got dressed picking the best clothes to wear during a murder. He only wore casual clothes so that was already decided. A hoodie and a pair of jeans would do for tonight's home invasion. He thought he'd compliment his outfit with a pair of grey Nike air max. He went straight to the kitchen with his hair still wet and whipped up a quick make do meal. Microwaved lasagne was on the menu, accompanied by some garlic. He gave Marley his favourite which was lamb and veg in jelly. The time was just turning five o clock and he was ready, ready to satisfy his need. The hot blades had eased off due to the pain killers he took before his five-star meal. He sat down thinking of a plan. How was he going to do this? He planned to spray the husband's car with spray paint, making himself known with a stone smashing a window would do the trick. Knowing the type of person her husband was, he will do two things. Chase him to teach him a lesson and get it repainted straight away, no one wants to drive around with the word 'TWAT' on their car. Mike smirked at the idea of him been sat behind the wheel driving a twat mobile. The clock read 5:20, he planned to get to smithies lane around 7 pm to suss everything out. He needed to work out an entry point to the home and an escape route which would divert him back to the house. He knew that the home had plenty of woodland around it so he would lose the husband in there. He'd then wait for his car to leave. That's then he'd make his way in and calm the storm brewing inside of him. He was going to enjoy turning out her lights. He couldn't wait to watch her fade into nothing. He stood up in excitement rubbing his hand. 'Come on Marls, let's go get some spray' the 7-year-old dog got up from his bed and walked to the door, Mike grabbed his leash and put it on his red leather collar. B&Q was only 10 minutes away. He planned to go a longer way around to give his only friend a good walk. 'You're not the only one who's getting something around they're neck tonight buddy' he said as if Christmas had come early.

CHAPTER EIGHT:

Mike loved Christmas time, he loved everything about it. The tree, the lights and he loved the true meaning which was his family. Mike truly loved his father. His dad had always taken a special interest in every part of his life. His father taught him how to play football, play pool and when the weather was right, he took him fishing to the pond in the small village of Carlton. The pond ran through the outskirts of the town. Flowing through Royston as well as Notton. Mike knew when his dad took him fishing things were a little heated between him and his mum. It was an escape route for them both to get out of the way of her psychotic episodes. The Christmas Mike would never forget was when he was just 7 years old. He was extremely excited because of what he had put on his list. A brand new fishing pole. He wanted to have a reason to spend time with just with his dad when his mother was going nuts about something small. If he had a rod, his dad had a reason to take him more. That Christmas morning at 6 am Mike raced downstairs to see that Santa had been. He stopped in amazement and inspected the living room. The tree was surrounded by presents. Every shape and size stood there just waiting to be opened by him. The joy on his face expressed his appreciation. The sense of everything he had wished for was in that room, well almost everything. The main thing Mike wanted was a mother who was nice to him. A mother who loved and cared for him instead of abusing him mentally and physically. His father knew about the chamber Mike used to get punished in, but he never dared argue with his dearest wife. Mike often wondered why they had a child. When he was in the chamber, he'd think that a lot. The darkness and the loneliness were his only true relationships he had in their care. That Christmas was no different. The clock struck the 1 pm mark and all their family had been and gone. They had all given the Ashburn family their presents and best wishes. It was just the three of them now. They all sat in the living room stuffed from the delicious moist turkey. His father was fast asleep in the chair with his mouth wide open. Like a hippo defending its territory. His mum sat in the armchair across from him watching songs of praise. Humming all the songs that were devoted to the lord and savior. Mike was eager to get back to the pond and learn everything there was about fishing. He wanted to know everything about his brand new anglers' pole. He just wanted to get away from her with his dad. The pair of them always bonded over the activity. The fresh air, the dirt, the umbrella which sheltered them from the elements. It was all perfect for Mike. It made him truly happy. But it was always ruined by a phone call from his mother telling his dad she needed a job doing. They would head home, and Mike would spend the rest of the day in his room if not the chamber. He went over to the Christmas tree, it stood just small enough to fit in the house without bending the top branch on the ceiling. Fully decorated with tinsel and brightly coloured baubles. The bitch has got something right he thought as he neared the tree. He glanced down to see the perfect fishing pole he could have ever had hoped for. The pole was surrounded by a variety of toys and books. All his favourite characters from the marvel universe scattered across the floor in a variety of sizes. Wolverine was Mike's favourite because of how brave and ruthless he was with his claws. He had the latest books from the marvel universe packed with stories of the Amazing Spider-man and the Incredible Hulk. Reading allowed Mike to escape his horrible reality. What better way to do it than reading about superheroes? He always imagined if he had the power of super-strength, he would grab his mother by the neck and throw her in the chamber and laugh as he asked how do you like it? He stared at the dark purple pole. It was a thing of beauty and he knew he had to take a lot of care of it. It was as precious as gold to Mike. He picked it up and held it steady. Examining the pole for any slight kinks in the smooth curved body. He grasped the base of the pole and imagined he had a fish hooked on the end. He started yanking at thin air, getting plenty of practice in for the canal. swooping from left to right his mother set her eyes on him. She was watching him like a Hawk. Mike could feel her eyes burning his skin, like candle wax dripping onto paper. He steadied his movement avoiding the ornaments which covered the fireplace. He waited a few seconds till her sight was fixed on the television once again. He stared at the floor and thought of being on the canal with his dad. The smell of the salt in the air and the cold on his face is what made him happy. The fresh air is what he missed the most while he was cooped up in the chamber. He started to sway again with the thought of a fishing trip running through his mind. The pole started to dip up and down. His eyes were shut tight. It was Christmas but it didn't feel like it. It never did. Christmas was always ruined by a heated argument followed by apologies from both sides of mum and dad. It was only a matter of time until his dad woke up and show would begin. The rod tapped a pale white clock ornament. His eyes shot open to see if his mother had noticed the tinging sound. She remained glued to the T.V. Mike was relieved. He tried to grasp the upper section of the pole. His heart sank when he grabbed thin air. The pole was on its way down to the ornament, his eyes grew wide as he watched it clatter the white clock. He knew what was coming as soon as that clock fell. He was fucked. It would be off to the chamber for the night and his mum and dad would argue for hours. He had to escape his reality, even if it was only for a few minutes. It was worth every moment spent in the chamber. The clock fell face forward to the ground. The smash it made on the solid tile floor was loud enough to wake his dad. His mother's head flung around fast enough to snap her neck in two. She glanced down at the shattered clock on the floor. Mike stood their holding his new pole in shock. He knew what was to come. Before he could apologise for the accident his mother had his arm firmly grasped. He looked at his dad for a lifeline, hoping for him to tell her to put him down, but he just stared at the floor. She dragged him to the staircase and flung the chamber door open. Mike always dreaded the part where he got thrown in, but he knew it was better than been out in the open when she was angry. She was like a snake with three thangs and too much venom when she was mad and his dad always felt the true power of her bite. Mike waited for the door to slam shut and welcomed the calming darkness. Christmas was ruined but at least he was safe. He knew he wasn't getting his arm broke like the Christmas before. He sat there in silence. Anxiety had taken over for a minute, but the calmness came. He knew one day he would have his revenge on his mother. He didn't know how but he would get it if it was the last thing he did. He felt safe in the chamber but that didn't mean he didn't hate it. He hated it just like he hated her existence.

'One day mother, you will pay.'

CHAPTER NINE:

Jack Brown was well known in the town as one of the lads. He was always polite and never arrested people for illegal activities when he was off duty. He needed to be liked by his fellow people. He went for a drink in the Blacksmith almost every day after he'd been to the office. He loved the craft beers they sold. He thought it would be best to keep a low profile and not draw attention to himself. After all, the Blacksmith was notorious for drugs and violence and even the odd case of unprotected sex in the men's toilet. The pub sat on the corner of the long-paved road which was Church Street, just opposite the town hall. The building was old, originally an old hotel built in the early 1900's, it stood pale white. It's stone texture was rough to the touch. Tab ends and empty glasses surrounded the perimeter of the pub. Its beer garden was always full in the summertime. The people of Barnsley liked to party, and the Blacksmith was the spot to go. Full of students and middle-aged adults, the scene was anyone's. Jack always sat at the same table, just off the entrance was a single table which faced the bar. He would go get a drink. Jack with a dash of coke and a huge ice cube was his favourite, he'd order and go sit down away from the beautiful people and relax. He would let all the worries and stress from the job just fade away with every sip. Jack lived alone. His two-bedroom house on Rye Croft avenue used to home three people but since his wife left with his daughter, it was just him. Since the new serial killer had come to the surface, he hadn't been getting a lot of sleep. Jack had never been on a case before with very little leads. The media wanted answers from the captain, and the captain wanted answers from him. He had none. The only thing he had to go on so far was the fact the killer defiantly hated women. Four women baring the same message of a snapped ring finger had to be a man's doing with a passion to see them dead. And the phone call Lauren made or answered the day she was found with her neck destroyed from the strangulation. Every sip of the jack and coke made the nightmare slip out of his mind, a little at a time. Four women and no leads, some cop you are Jack he thought to himself as he shook his head.

'Hey baby, how you doing?'

Jack turned his head immediately left to see a woman stood no more than 2 feet away from him. Her brunette hair sat on her shoulders like a parrot waiting for a cracker. The brown hair made her facial features impossible to miss. Her bright green eyes complimented her cherry red lips. Jack's eyes scanned every inch of her perfectly sculpted body. Her huge rack and her round ass were crying for his attention and he couldn't help but stare.

'you on your own, sweetie?' she said fluttering her eyes.

'Yeah, unfortunately. I'm always on my own.' He replied thinking how sad he sounded. He also added a wink to try and seal the deal. He didn't even know her name and he was desperate to bed the look-alike model. It had been so long since he'd had the company of a lady, he had forgotten which one it was who supposed to be tied up. That didn't matter, a quickie in the toilets would have given him all the satisfaction he needed.

'aw boo, such a shame, a sexy man like yourself all alone, what do you say I change that?' She asked followed by the raising of the eyebrows.

'Yes please.' He said. Hoping he didn't sound desperate. He necked his drink finishing the strong fiery liquid in one gulp. He shot out of his chair and took her hand.

'Come on, let's get you a real drink' He said with an overpowering smile. The hurried off out of the doors and into the rain. They glanced at one another. Desperately craving each other, they couldn't walk fast enough. Their smiles and their thoughts about the sex what was to come was loudly interrupted by the screech of Jack's iPhone 7. The number was the office number and he knew what it was about. Before he went for a drink and met the possible prostitute, he had Sarah Johnson run Lauren's phone call records. She worked a lot of overtime, mainly because she enjoyed and got a good rush from helping people. It was a shame she never made it as a cop, Jack always thought she would have made a good partner. He answered the call after the third ring.

'Detective Jack Brown, speaking?' He asked.

'Jack, it's Sarah. I've ran the records from 12-4PM like you asked.'

'Hey Sarah, any luck?' his gut told him it was bad news. This case was nothing but bad news.

'It's bad news, Jack. There are not any calls from that time zone you requested.'

'Ah shit, when was the last call made by her?' he asked hoping for something.

'The last call was made at 5 past 8 in the morning to the sandwich box, guessing she ordered breakfast. Sorry, Jack.' Her voice was quiet as she explained the bad news. She desperately wanted it to be good news for him. Not just to get her rush from being helpful but to get a step closer to bringing the son of a bitch down. The monster who was murdering women for no apparent reason.

He looked at the stunning woman that stood before him with a sad look on his face.

'Son of a bitch.' He whispered. 'Ok, thank you, Sarah" the line went dead. He put his phone in his pocket and turned around and started walking.

'Hey, are we doing this or...?' she shouted as he walked off in anger. He stopped dead in his tracks and spun around to face her perfectly sculpted body.

'Fuck off' he said with a pause in the words to add emphasis on his insult. He turned around and set off again heading to another bar he knew where he could kill his brain cells in peace.

'Wanker!' she screamed at the top of her lungs. Jack wasn't in the mood for fucking, he wanted to be left alone. The only thing he couldn't get out of his mind was why would Mike Ashburn tell him false information about something so serious? Tomorrow he would go to his depot and ask him in person. The only reason he could think of was that Mike Ashburn knew more than he let on about Lauren or he was hiding something. Something about Lauren or something about the Snapper.

CHAPTER TEN:

The rain had started again. Bouncing off the tarmac. Smithies lane had a river flowing down the left side of the road. The dark grey sky was lashing the earth with its daggers. Another month's worth of rain would fall for sure on this night. The night the 5th would finally have her lights turned out. Mike had been to the local B&Q for a can of yellow spray paint for the douche bags car. He chose yellow because it would be harder to miss, giving him every reason to protect his ego even more. He had taken Marley home, he didn't want to get in him any danger. He valued his dog very much. He had already organised for him to be taken by the police and given training if anything was to happen to a Mr Mike Ashburn, He had to make sure Marley was taken care off. He also picked up a pair of black leather gloves from the charity shop Barnardo's a few days ago. After his fourth victim, he decided he needed to take a little more care with his killing. After watching the hit T.V. show Dexter, he felt he picked up a few pointers. Gloves to hide his prints and a patient attitude to his kills were what he needed. He strolled down towards the bottom of Smithies Lane. The rain landed on the peak of his hood and started to drip onto his face. He always found comfort in the poor weather. Just like the chamber, it made him feel safe. The coldness made him feel numb, the same numbness from his childhood. Mike was ecstatic, it was finally the night of the 5th, he'd been ready for this for a while. The storm was on the brink of arrival and he needed to satisfy it quick. He hated the migraines which would follow. The pain was so unboreable it made him kill someone. That and an appearance from the bitch herself. He walked with a bit more pace to his steps as he neared the poorly lit stone house. He could start to make out the woodland area around it. His escape route for both acts of the evening. After he sprayed the car, he would get his attention while he was at the end of his drive and sprint into the darkness hoping he would follow. Mike knew he would, his material items are far too precious to him. He would defiantly want to kill the asshole who thinks it's funny to spray paint someone's property. Mike stopped on the corner of the lane under an old oak tree. He took out a cigarette and sparked it up. The delicious smoke shot down his lungs to calm his nerves. It had been a while since his last kill, he was nervous. Nervous but excited. The storm kept nagging and nagging to be calmed. The migraine had kicked up with a fire behind his eyes. The pain was bearable, but he knew it would get worse if he didn't act. He took a long second drag on the cigarette butt. Looking into the sky in the rain shining as it fell from the clouds. The rain and the grey sky reminded him of his father. They would sit on the riverbank in the same weather for hours. The weather was the reason they bonded under the umbrella. Sheltered from the daggers they would talk about family life and mainly his mother. He'd ask questions his father couldn't answer. He would change the subject to football or Mike's interests. He didn't mind but he wanted answers to why he had to go in the chamber, but they never came. He stopped his thoughts and concentrated on his smoke. He glanced down the lane to see the lights on in most of the rooms. The windows illuminated the branches of his escape route. The thought of him finally getting to turn off the lights was overwhelming. He finished his fag and flicked on the wet ground. He couldn't wait any longer. He checked his phone to see the time was 6:36 PM. He had waited long enough, and it was finally showtime. He rearranged the can of paint in the back pocket of his blue Levi jeans and set off almost power walking to his next victims' home.

CHAPTER ELEVEN:

Mike had clapped his eyes on the car from the trees in the darkness. He had lit up another smoke to smooth the excitement of been mischievous.

'I need to cut down on these things.' He uttered as he exhaled. The black land rover was a beautifully crafted car, it was riding on huge high-end alloys valued at least £2000 each. He could see the cream seats inside the vehicle which meant only one thing. Those seats were also expensive. They had rollers inside and came with a specialised remote to choose your function. It could either massage or lay almost flat for your comfort needs. Its huge headlights reminded him of a monster's eye. He wouldn't want to be spotted by the LED lights. It could easily light up the woodland with ease, which wasn't good. He needed to be gone in a flash. The car was facing the woods, Mike needed to be a ghost in this master plan of his. He needed to be invisible. No one could know he'd even been on smithies lane. As soon as he would leave to get his car sorted, he would emerge from the woods and strangle her with pure force and snap her finger to fulfill his need. It was time, he had waited long enough for this moment. He slipped on his leather gloves and shuffled through the shrubs. He stood up straight under the tallest lamppost he'd ever seen in Barnsley. He sprinted to cover behind an electric box. The dark green metal camouflaged perfectly in the darkness. He started to breathe heavy. The adrenalin had kicked in already making his skin crawl with weakness. His head began to become hot and he was short of breath. He took a minute to perk himself with a pep talk.

'Come on Mike, it's fucking time' he said in anger. He knew it was her or he would lose his mind. He couldn't face another haunting from the witch, his mother. He had to act or go down in flames. He peeked over the box and assessed the surroundings. There was no one in sight. The house next door had its dining room light on but that didn't worry him. He would be as quiet as a mouse. No one would know who it was other than the one the media called The Snapper. Mike hated that name, he had thought of writing a letter to the South Yorkshire police taunting them how they couldn't catch him like Jack the Ripper did. He would sign with a different name, but he didn't dare. He couldn't take the risk of it being traced back to him, so The Snapper had to do. He looked at the house and examined the property for any form of light. The downstairs was lit up like the sky on the 4th of July he thought. The upstairs landing and all the bedrooms were darker than the woods. He needed to get closer to make sure they were both home, otherwise, this was a huge waste of his time. He snuck out of the trees trying not to make a sound as if they could hear him through the double-glazed glass of their bay window. He tiptoed as quietly as he could. The rain was louder than anyone's footsteps, but Mike was taking no chances. Slowly but surely, he thought as he crept from the shadows. He arrived at his destination just on the opposite side of their garden wall. The entrance to the woods was no more than 7ft away from where he was. It was almost too perfect he could disappear with ease. His all-black outfit (except his grey AirMax) would increase his chances of not getting spotted in the trees and the shadows. He knelt behind the wall trying to pluck up the courage to peek his head out. He had a feeling he was going to get spotted. It was just his luck to be denied his 5th victim. He craved her body to be a corpse by the time he left here on this night. He slowly peeked over the wall to find he couldn't see them. He could see the two cars parked getting lashed by the rain. But no people.

'Going to need a better view' He whispered to himself. The height of the bay window meant he couldn't see over into the dining room. The angle was obtuse. He scanned the environment for a better position. He noticed a gap in the wall where the gate was. The fact he could be seen crossing the foot of the open wall terrified, but he couldn't be bothered to return into the shadows. He shimmied along the dirt with his hand guiding him along the rough brick wall. He took his time and took extra care not to slip and cause himself an injury, but the rain made sure it was a challenge. The mud felt like it was a landslide. He approached the opening. He poked one half of his face to check the coast was clear. Nothing but the two cars. He quickly shot across, keeping low camouflaging into the dirt. He slammed on the breaks and brought his movement to complete halt, almost slipping in the process.

'Hard parts done.' He said with a chuckle. He carried on walking in the crouched position until he reached the end of the wall and took cover behind the huge pillar. He took a moment to gather his feelings and tried to contain them. He needed to calm down and compose himself. He had done this before, so why was he so nervous? This would be his 5th victim, he knew how it felt, he knew how to do it almost to perfection he thought but something wasn't right. Something was bugging him. All his victims were married so there wasn't anything different he thought. They all were strangled, all got the trademark of his kill, all the same way, all in purpose to calm the storm. Then it hit him. This was the first time he had to get the husband out of the way first. This one the 5th was more of a risk, more chance of getting found out. The police and the news had told the public to issue a report of any strange activity like someone creeping in your garden and defiantly if someone spray paints your car. Mike was hoping he was too stuck up to call the cops. He knew he was an asshole who thought he was the man. He could tell that just by the car he drove. He lit up a cigarette, his 3rd in the space of half an hour. The nicotine helped with excitement and brought him back down to earth. He gathered his thoughts and thought of the ways he could get caught. He went through every detail of his scenario's and he decided to take extra care and time. Use the darkness and the rain to his advantage. Adapt any way he could to get the best result. He wasn't a religious man, but he was sure if hell was real. He had a place reserved for him and his evil tendencies. Right next to Hitler and the priest who used to come to his school and look up the little girl's skirts. He nipped out his smoke and peeked around the pillar, he could see the kitchen window to see the husband standing there having a smoke through the window. Blowing it through the crack in the bevel. He did a quick scan for the reason he was here, but there was no sign of the bitch. The upstairs was in the dark. He couldn't make out where the upstairs windows were, but he could just see the fascia board below the roof tiles. The water was dripping down like a waterfall. The weather was getting worse and worse by the minute. Mike was getting cold. It was 4 degrees, this was the sign he had to move. If he stayed crouch his legs would lock up and he'd be there until morning.

'Let's do this' he said to himself. The storm was on the horizon and his migraine was kicking up a fuss and starting to irritate him. He shuffled himself around the corner of the pillar and revealed himself to the open driveway. The most vulnerable the Snapper had ever been. He darted across the pale concrete and took shelter under the kitchen window, hoping the husband didn't notice him. He decided to wait a few minutes to see if he came out with a weapon, that would be the reasonable response to a hooded figure creeping on their property. The Land Rover was just a few feet away to his right-hand side. He rested his hand and his left ear on the cold red bricks. Hoping to hear someone on the other side of the cavity wall. They'd be closer than he would like but at least he would know their location. a minute went by like an hour, stuck in the same crouching position he had been in for the last twenty minutes. He finally heard a cough. It wasn't clear more of an echo, so he guessed it came from the hallway or the living room. He stood up and teased the top half of his head over the window cill. No sign of anyone, all the lights lit the way to the living room. The dark wooden floor was spotless. This would be a problem for marks and fingerprints. Luckily, he brought his leather gloves. The kitchen was a new modern style with plenty of cupboards and storage units covering the walls. He guessed that the fridge and the freezer was also part of the modern design. The dishwasher was defiantly the star of the family. The glasses and dirty plates were lined up like soldiers on one of the sides, but the sink was bone dry of water and pots. This was the chance to get into position. The rear of the car was just in sight of the bay window. If he went around the front and kept low, he'd be out of sight until he started making a racket. He followed through on his thought and did his manoeuvre in less than five seconds. He was there. Facing the passenger door, he looked at the water droplets running down the black metal. The cold wind blew up the back of his top and on to his neck making his hair stand on end. Reminding him to act quickly not only to get his 5th victim but to keep warm. England was well known for its cold weather, but lately, South Yorkshire dominated the headlines with a new killer at large. Little did they know Barnsley would be in the news again in the morning as the Snapper was close to having a 5th victim.

CHAPTER TWELVE:

Jack was sitting alone at a VIP seating area of the Swivel bar. It was packed, Wednesday was student night around Barnsley and anyone who is in education after secondary was out. Drug use and alcohol abuse happened almost every night but on Wednesday's and Saturday's was the emergency services busiest night. Jack was sat nursing a pint. The table was huge and perfectly round, also a little sticky from all the spilled lager, ideal for big parties of people. The table was full of empty beer bottles and crystals of powder, but Jack wasn't bothered. He didn't care that the club was full of people doing illegal activities. what bothered him was he had nothing on the Snapper. The people here partying were in a controlled environment and they were not out killing innocent people. Four bodies in three months and not a single fibre of clothing had been left behind, Jack was lost. He couldn't reassure his captain never mind the public. All he knew was someone had purposely lied about one of the victims. Why would Mike

Ashburn tell him that he saw her on her phone when he knew he'd find out the truth. The only explanation was she had a second secret phone to deal with all the bad stuff in her life. He needed to speak to Mike urgently, try to catch him off guard if he was hiding something. The music was overwhelming. The bass from the speakers were attacking Jack's eardrums so he decided to call it a night, it was late enough anyway. He started his shift at 8 AM sharp and he needed some sleep. He necked the rest of the hops larger and headed to the door. He made his way through the busy dance floor, dodging all the young beautiful people with great difficulty. He made it to the stairs which led down to the exit. He couldn't wait to taste the fresh air. The six pints was overpowering, and he could feel himself feeling a little on the sick side. He headed down the steep mountain like steps, passed the bouncer and the entry point and out into the rain. He took a moment and hoped his dizziness would ease while the cold water poured on to his face. He stepped back under the cover of the entrance to the bar and pulled out his phone. The phone lit up and displayed a photo of his daughter on her 7th birthday. Every time Jack unlocked his phone, he felt sad. That picture always reminded him of what was missing at home. his wife left him the moment she found out about his affair. The one-night stand happened 3 years ago while he was sent to Birmingham to help on a case. The Sargent owed a favour to an old friend, one thing led to another, a serial killer was on his cycle of sending out messages to the city and Jack had to go catch him. He spent 6 months away living in a hotel room. The night before they caught the son of a bitch Jack's stress was getting on top of him. She was there in the bar flirting, laughing and sending out a signal she was interested. By the morning they woke up in his room naked. Jack was full of lost memories of the night but most of all he was full of shame. After the killer was arrested and taken into custody, he headed home. he lied for three weeks before he slipped up. He was showing her a photo of his hotel and she swiped right again to reveal a photo of him and the average looking woman. She was devasted. She listened to his bullshit excuses, but she was too smart to be taken for a fool. The day after she was gone. She took his daughter with her to go live with her parents in Sheffield. He understood and did nothing regarding custody. He had caused enough damage to them both. He sees his daughter on the weekends and the last Thursday of every month while his ex-wife goes to her monthly yoga class. He redialled Sarah's number and stopped himself pressing the call icon. She would be asleep by now he thought so a text for the morning would do.

Hey Sarah, call me in the morn it's urgent JB. Read the message. He hit send and headed home. he wanted one thing off the helpful office clerk. A background check on a Mr M Ashburn should shed some light on what kind of person he was. It was also so he wouldn't go in blind to his next interview with Mike and this time he'll know when he's lying. He started to pick up the pace in the heavy rain. His clothes began to weigh him down. His house was a few miles away from the town centre. He lived in Strawberry Gardens in the village of Royston. He bought the house when he was 25 and lived alone by the time he was 30. His well-paid salary meant he didn't have to sell up. He grew fond of the huge three bedded home. it was his little oasis since his wife left him. It had acquired a pool table and a two-seater bar to comfort his loneliness. Most nights he didn't even make it up to his bedroom. He spent most of his nights on the sofa hugging a bottle of vodka and his dog Max. Max had become his whole world over cheap alcohol and dirty acts with women. He loved spending time with him, most work nights he spent watching sports with Max. A couple of beers and an ordered in pizza with an action movie or live Premier league football is what made his day. Other than snapping the cuffs on someone who deserved it. He missed them both a great deal, but Max had filled some of the void deep inside him, but deep down he enjoyed his new lifestyle. The booze and the women took first place over his daughter, he loved her dearly, but like her mother used to say, not enough.

He had been stumbling in the rain for a good 15 minutes and he finally reached his gate to his drive. His car stood firm in the drenched tarmac. He knew the risks of drink driving so he always left it behind, he didn't fancy his chances. If he got caught intoxicated behind the wheel it was game over. Sargent Dickson would have his balls for dinner. He walked down the drive and down the dark path which led to his door. The door swung open and Jack flung himself inside. He was grateful for the instant warmth which blasted him. He tried to compose himself and work out where he was. The liquor and the cold rain had sent his senses all over the place. A few seconds passed and he finally came back to earth. He stood in his kitchen, the rain bouncing off the window. His sleeves were dripping on the black tiled floor almost turning it into a hazard. He had one thought on his mind and that was his bed. He was so tired, he was tired of being tired. Ever since the fourth victim was discovered five days ago, he had no more than 8 hours of sleep. The Snapper was haunting him in every way he could. In his dreams and in his reality. The Sargent was becoming desperate for answers. As he piled the pressure on him, the more he became more disconnected from the case. His interests were mainly focused on alcohol and women lately. He headed upstairs stumbling over every step. He emptied his pockets on to his desk spewing out his keys and his ID. He threw his jacket on the floor and jumped into bed fully clothed. He turned on to his back and began to stare at the ceiling. He couldn't bring himself to think of the Snapper, but he was always there. In the back of his mind creeping in his brain. Jack couldn't help but feel like he was responsible for the four dead women, he couldn't catch the guy. He knew another woman's life was at risk, and with no leads, it was inevitable that a new victim would surface very soon. He had a hunch that Mike Ashburn knew more about Lauren than he let on. Why would someone provide false information to the police other than to hide something? But what was he hiding? The question ran around in his head as he tried to sleep but he could tell it was going to be another all-nighter. He tended to question everything. That was his job after all as a detective. Just like every good cop they never knew how to switch off. He felt his head getting heavier and sink deeper into his pillow. It was the night he would finally get sleep. He couldn't help but smile a little as he started to drift off. His drift was interrupted by his phone alerting him that he had a call. Jack shot up in shock as if someone broke in and headed towards his jacket laying on the floor. He searched the insides pockets and found his iPhone. The displayed said Sarah to his disbelief. He answered in his tired voice.

'Sarah, it's very late what's up?'

'Jack! I'm sorry for calling so late but it's urgent and you need to know before you question Mike again.' Her sentence came to a holt as she ran out of breath.

'Go on, I'm listening.' He replied.

'Mike's parents, his dad was found dead in his home after he had been strangled and his mother is completely off the radar. She was last seen in 2012 the day before his dad was found dead. On the 7th of February, she was seen walking into the house with a shovel in her hand by a neighbour and the day after she was a ghost. I hope this gives you the upper hand and catches him off guard. Maybe you will see his true colours.'

'Sarah, thank you' He hung up and realised the instant connection. Mike's dad found dead by been strangled, the snapper strangles women and Mike giving him false information. It was not looking good the bin man. He was hiding something, and he had just shot straight up to the top of his suspect list.

CHAPTER THIRTEEN:

Five minutes had passed, and Mike was still crouched behind the car. The rain had no sign of stopping but he didn't mind. His legs were numb he had been crouched for that long, he needed to act soon otherwise he would not be able to move quickly and efficiently in the house. He slowly stood up but stayed in a crouched position, so he was still hidden behind the land rover. He felt his back pocket for the can of spray and grabbed it. He began to spray the side which was not visible from the house. The word TWAT in huge letters covered 90% of the doors. Mike wanted to make sure he'd be pissed. To make sure he would be chased. He sprayed his side mirror with the yellow paint. Impairing his vision of the road while he drove, just for fun. Mike never met the dude be he couldn't help but hate him. He always hated people like him. Self-centered, arrogant and selfish. Those men were the worst. Troy was one of those guys, Mike felt like he acted the way he did on purpose to annoy him. But he knew he didn't, he acted that way because he was selfish. Self-centered. He couldn't be without attention. His everyone look at me attitude would eventually make him flip and he knew it. He'd never killed a man before, but he was looking forward to strangling Troy. Deep down he had a minor ounce of hate for him. He pulled his finger off the can and admired his original Michelangelo piece. The words twat and prick splashed on the black bodywork of the £30,000 car. Mike felt proud. He scurried low along the ground and headed to the boot of the car. He paused and looked at all the windows. They were all emerged in darkness except the downstairs kitchen window which shun a little light from the living room. He was clear to proceed. He gripped the spray-paint can tightly, channeling his anger into the can. He could feel his blood start to boil as he felt a throb from the back of his head. It was on its way and Mike knew it. The migraine would be in full flow in around ten minutes. He knew he had to act quickly if he was to calm the storm. The last thing he wanted was to have to see her face. Her face haunted him ever since he was a little boy. A small fragile boy locked away under the stairs not knowing what he had done wrong most of the time.

He pushed the top of the can to release the thick liquid from the can. The boot was the target this time. Mike thought a huge penis would do. It would defiantly make him go out of his way to rectify the paint job. He knew he couldn't be seen driving a luxury car full of swear words and huge dicks. He finished the artwork and gathered his thoughts. He looked up to the sky for an answer on what his next move was, but the reply was just huge rain droplets. His head began to pulsate at a steady pace, matching his heart rate. He took deep breathes to try and ease the pain and it seemed to work. He had one side left to complete before a brick would go through the window and he would get his 5th. The left side of the vehicle faced the kitchen window, making this a difficult task. If one of the occupants were to see him it was game over. He decided to head back to the bonnet and have a smoke before tackling the uneasy task. He pulled out a soggy lambert and butler gold and sparked the lighter. He lit it up and took a deep breath. The smoke shot down into his lungs like a knife and he had an instant rush of nicotine. He took his time with the cigarette and thought about his hand wrapped around her neck. Her sweet looking facial features would turn blue with Mike's hate. Her mouth would be open as wide as it could go, gasping for air, and Mike would smile with joy. He would then snap her finger back and the sound of the bone-crunching inside the skin would give him a shiver of satisfaction. He took his last draw and flicked his cigarette butt under the swear mobile. He peeked over the bonnet and checked the windows again. The coast was clear, and he was ready. He slid around the corner of the car like a ninja. He stopped dead in his tracks, and he was so close to the door he was almost hugging it. He pulled his can and applied the correct amount of pressure and began to spray. This side would host a childlike drawing of a jungle cat. Because why not he thought. Mike thought it would be hilarious for all the other road users.

Not only would he have a huge penis and absurd swear words. A stupid looking jungle cat would just put him over the edge. He stopped spraying and leaned back. His eyes met those of the artwork, and he couldn't help but laugh. Even he was shocked by how bad it was. He quickly darted across to the wall he hid behind. He was still on their driveway on the opposite side this time. He scouted the wet floor for any type of brick, stone or heavy object. Something strong enough to break glass. He came up empty. He decided to check the other side of the wall, he didn't want to end up having to go to the woods for something to break the window. He was too lazy, and he had to run for his life as soon as it was broke. He vaulted the old brick wall and landed in a muddy puddle. The bottom of his black Primark jeans had a bit of dirt on them, but he didn't notice. He was focused on finding a stone to throw. He searched the darkness and the slop for a few seconds and hand brushed over something hard. An old London brick was stuck deep in the mud. Mike grabbed it with both hands and pulled as hard as he could eventually prying It free. He held it like a new-born, this was his ticket to the 5th. Like Charlie holding his golden ticket. He started to become overwhelmed with excitement. Like a kid at a toy store. He turned back around and vaulted over the wall. He sprinted towards the house, not even checking if anyone could see his figure in the shadows. He pulled his arm back as far as it could go, and he threw the brick like a professional shot-put champion. He watched it glide through the air. Cutting the oxygen like a knife through butter. With a loud smash, it crashed through the kitchen window, shattering the glass into a thousand pieces.

'Showtime.' He whispered in a happy voice.

CHAPTER FOURTEEN:

Ben and Troy never missed a Wednesday night on the town. Student night was very popular for all age groups. Anyone's chance to get laid. That's why Troy was there. Their night started at Ben's place with a crate of Fosters to share. They would make sure it was gone by 7 PM and they would head into the town to see all the beautiful people. They'd start in the Olde. Notorious for the wrong crowd but famous for cheap booze. They'd sink a few pints, have a bag of crisps when the beer munchies kicked in and head over to the Blacksmith. This was the place for the students to meet up and have a good time with each other. Full of world-famous beers and ales. A delicious menu perfect for any occasion and a fresh coat of paint made it one of Barnsley's must-go places. Ben was stood at the bar. The old-timer looked out of place, but he didn't mind. He never did when his bloodstream was 75% Fosters. He raised his arm with a £10 note dangling from his hand to insinuate he needed serving. A young barman saw the gesture and walked over.

'Yes mate?' asked the young prodigy. His young boyish charm caught Ben off guard. His perfectly ironed shirt just sat above his Gucci belt. His straight brown quiff just sat above his blue eyes making him just Ben's type. Ben was recently divorced, when he told his wife he was gay she left the same day. He never knew it until a year ago when he found himself in the bed of property manager of Barnsley council. They had met at work in the break room (just like Mike and Lauren) and bumped into each other in the Joseph to Joseph. They had a drink with each other, and one thing led to another. Ben remembers it being a beautiful moment for him as a person. He had learned something about himself he never even thought could be possible. He woke up that morning, well-rested. The smell of cinnamon and toast filled the bedroom he had slept in. He came around from his 12-hour sleep and smiled. The first time he had smiled in months up until that point. He had breakfast and then left the perfect man. James had his mortgage paid off by the time he was 25, so he told Ben. His job had its perks, a brand-new car every 2 years, flash suits and the rich lifestyle fitted him like a slipper. The young man had been to college to study English literature, but he quit. He found it boring and he didn't want to be in thousands and thousands of pounds of debt. He always wanted to be rich like his father. So, he used him to his advantage. His dad had been with the council 17 years, he retired that year James quit and showed him the ropes about property. Then when his father finally retired, he walked into the job. 3 years later he had done well for himself, got promotion after promotion and finally got the manager's job just like his dad. Ben didn't know what to make of that, it happened all too fast, but he thought he had pulled a good one considering it was his first.

'Can I get two Vodka red bulls please?' Asked Ben slurring his words. The 15 pints had killed a few of his brain cells but he was still standing. He always powered through trying to keep up with Troy. He was a lot younger than Ben, his life outside work was beer. It had been since he was in school, so his tolerance was high, especially for a 25-year-old. His favourite drink was a single malt whiskey. He loved how it made his hair stand on the back of his neck. The barman had just finished pouring the last drink and headed back to Ben. He carefully placed the drinks on the bar just in front of him and said

'£12.50' he gazed at Ben waiting for him to put his hand in his pocket since he was only holding a single ten. He did and threw some change on the bar. Hopefully, it was enough to pay the tab.

'Is that enough gorgeous?' Ben shut his trap as soon as he realised what he had said. Hoping he hadn't heard his compliment. The barman nodded and walked slowly back to the till. Relief washed over Ben. He only ever felt like this when he had had a few.

'I think you got away with it.' Said a deep female voice from behind the drunk bin man. The woman was holding an empty Strongbow cider glass which was empty. She was ready for another drink her stern look said. Ben turned around with his eyes blinking at different times.

'You okay sir?' she asked. Ben was almost out of it.

'I'm ok darling.' His best impression of a sober man was top-notch when he wanted it to be. 'All I want is my precious Vodka Red Bulls ha.' He explained. Praying she didn't bring up his cheesy compliment. He grabbed his drinks and made his way back to Troy before she questioned or insinuated on his sexuality. 'See ya love.' He said with a smile walking past her. He clapped eyes on Troy's slouching body and laughed. Boy, would he be worried when he saw what Ben had in his hand.

'Not I see you first Ben.' Whispered the woman to herself. She stood at the bar elegant for a 54-year-old woman. Face full of wrinkles and her hair perfectly red and straight. Light make-up to compliment her features and a nice smart casual outfit with black boots. She stood at the bar with a fiver in her fingers.

'Yes, love.' Said the young man.

'Pint of Strongbow please.' She handed her used glass in to be used again.

'Anything else?'

'Yes, do you know someone called Mike Ashburn?'

CHAPTER FIFTEEN:

Mike stood in the centre of the driveway with his hood up, ready to sprint at the first sign of any of the residents. He had heard shouting and rummaging coming from inside the property. The storm had kicked up a bigger fuss ever since he had shattered the glass. He was ready. He would wait all night if he had to. The 5th was just a couple of metres away and he wanted her bad. His migraine to his surprise had died down and took shelter. But Mike still felt the need to kill.

'OI, YOU!' Yelled a voice from the kitchen window. The man was raging like a bull. He vaulted the broken window and into the driveway joining Mike. Mike smiled from the darkness of his hooded jacket. 'You're fucking dead.' He started galloping towards him, saliva and water been thrown from his perfectly round head. He looked left to see what he had done to his precious automobile. Without stopping to check if it still worked, he picked up the pace, but Mike was quick on his toes. The man was roughly the same size and weight, but Mike was faster.

'Come here!' Yelled the bull-like creature. Mike was out of the garden and making his way down the dark twisting path which led to the woods. He ran lowering his body of the trees he noticed which were at head height. He believed his chaser wouldn't know this information and was hoping he would get hit square on in the jaw. He was right. Mike turned and face him once he was clear of the shrubs and low hanging trees. The first branch hit him on his forehead, not doing much damage. The second, however, hit him at a much faster pace. Busting his nose and sending him on his ass down the slippery slope. Mike turned and ran, sprinted more like. He had to circle the house and get into position so he could see the man leave to hopefully fix the twat mobile. So far, the pan was a good one, he just had to shake him in the woods.

The man picked himself up out of the soup like mud and held his nose tight. Hoping to stop the blood which was pissing out like a tap. His white T-shirt and grey jogging bottoms were completely written off. Just like he was. He steadily began to make his way back west to his home, feeling sorry for himself. Mike was still sprinting as fast as he could go. He knew those cigarettes were a bad idea, but his nerves seemed to kick into overdrive when he was doing something evil or bad. He panted his way through the dark woods. The area was almost black. Some dead bodies in here he thought as he neared the other end of the house. Would I ever dump a body in some woods? I would if I had to, he told himself. Giving himself lessons on killing was a favourite pass time of his. As he dreamed of Killing the woman from Smithies Lane he arrived at his checkpoint and hid behind the wall. Luckily the wall ran all around the edge of the house giving him plenty of hiding spots. He took out his pack of smokes and lit one, again. He scanned the house and saw the man limping into the house through the front door. 'So far, so good.' He reassured himself. Hoping he would come out with car keys.

'What the fuck?' his wife stood there in shock holding a plate supporting a sandwich she had made herself. 'Well…' she waited for a reply.

'Don't fucking ask.' Pure anger in his voice warned not to pry. He edged his way into the kitchen, using the walls as crutches. He made it without falling from his dead leg and sat at the breakfast bar pulling out his wet phone. He rang a number from his contacts and waited before saying 'Marty, it's James. Need a huge favour.' Marty was a specialist in Barnsley at paint jobs and when he heard what had happened to poor James, he saw the perfect opportunity to steal some cash from his "loyal customer."

'I'll pay that, not too bad I guess.' He hung up and went back to the hallway. He picked up an old jacket. It looked a bear had mauled it thinking it was a Red Salmon. He went out into the pouring rain and rushed to his Land Rover. He flung open the driver's side and quickly chucked the old flea-ridden jacket on the cream seat. Covering it so he wouldn't get mud all over his precious luxury way to travel. (Forgetting about the car mats) He started the engine and began to back out of the drive. In Mike's amazement, the plan had worked. His victim was just over that wall and a couple of feet away. The excitement was toxic. He smiled so wide his cheek muscles had cramped up. The 'Snapper' would be back in the headlines in a couple of hours.

CHAPTER SIXTEEN:

Mike ran like Mo Farah on a final lap towards the busted window. His entry point to the 5th was staring him square on in the face. He calmed and collected himself the best he could. But he couldn't wait. The storm was on the horizon and he had no interest to see how much thunder would echo in his mind. His need had to be satisfied, now. He grasped the bottom Bevel of the window and carefully climbed inside of the cold property. He didn't check for neighbours been nosey or if anyone was outside. He thought anyone willing to be out in this storm was truly mad. A little like him. His first mistake, but he hoped it wouldn't cost him. He landed silently. Light on his feet like a cat. Not a creek had come out of the floor. He did a quick scan and heard a T.V screeching laughter and the voice of Michael Macintyre coming from upstairs. 'Perfect.'

He slowly made his way through the shadows and rubbed his hands together, gently. Warming them up so he would be able to feel her smooth skin as he squeezed the life out of her. The simple thought sent shivers of ecstatic through his body. The photographs hanging dormant on the walls displayed family life. Love and laughter could be heard in the hallway. Something Mike had never known. His mother had destroyed all those chances for him to be happy. Anger began to creep up his spine. Sending his fuse into overdrive. He scowled at the picture of a child laughing on the douchebag's shoulders and punched it shattering the glass. This made him feel a little better until he heard the voice from upstairs say 'Hello?'

He quietly retreated to the kitchen rubbing his sore knuckles. The stairs began to creak and squeak as a force made the descent into Mike's fury. It was time. The 5th, so close he could already hear her begging for her murder to stop. For it to be over. He was ready. Five days without a kill. The need was becoming more frequent, but he would satisfy himself until someone stopped him. No one ever cared about him, so why should he? He saw a hand take hold of the banister as she arrived at the downstairs portion of the house. The figure stopped moving. Mike was crouched ready to rush at her as soon as she turned that corner. 'Hello?' called out the voice another time. This one was more assertive and sent a warning to any trespasser. Surely, she was going to check the kitchen since the window had been smashed he thought clenching his fists, dreaming of a smoke. A smoke sounded good right about now. Especially with a breath of fresh air. He noticed he began to feel anxious as she had control of this moment.

'Come on, come on.' He said under his breath. The hand let go of the banister and the figure entered the hallway. Taking no notice of the smashed photograph. Mike set off quicker than a cheetah hunting a wildebeest. Her eyes widened in shock as she noticed the intruder. Mike was so close as she began to spin around on the spot. As he grabbed her neck, she was facing the front door, desperately reaching out for the handle to maybe escape, but he had her. He squeezed her thin neck so tight she couldn't even let out a scream, not even a little yelp. Joy washed over him like a warm Caribbean wave. He dragged her into the living room and threw her across the wooden floor. She gasped her airflow wasn't restricted anymore. Taking huge inhales and trying to come back to reality, Mike jumped on top of her. He grabbed her neck once more and hit her head as hard as he could on the cold floor. Smirking as he squeezed her. Her arms and legs were waving in the air for anything. Anything she could reach would be ideal as a weapon, but her OCD had betrayed her. The whites of her eyes began to turn red as she was deprived of oxygen, veins slowly popping out of her forehead. As she lay there been strangled by the Snapper, thoughts flashed of all the things she would have done differently. She would have made it work with James, she would have been a better mother to Jake and most importantly she would have followed through on her promise to her late father, to expose the council of their budget-cutting and tax robbing ways. But all that had disappeared. Her existence had disappeared as the Snapper had done what he set out to do. Jake was motherless and James was wifeless. All the happy times they had in their home would become a nightmare. A burial ground where their darling Loraine had been murdered for no apparent reason. What was something beautiful and sacred, was now dark and full of evil. Mike stood up and took hold of her wedding finger, snapping the finger like a twig. He felt reborn. He caressed the wedding ring and stared into the Gold. All he saw was unhappiness and lies. Just like his mother would portray her family. The front door opened and to Mike's surprise heard a voice utter 'Babe?'

'Oh fuck.' Mike darted through a little out cove and to the back wall in the dining room in a blind panic, not knowing which way to go or which way was up, he took cover behind the fancy oak wood table. Hosting 6 seats and plenty of conversation starters. The cutlery had to be of the 20th century. The fancy paintings hanging on the wall, some classic styles with a healthy mix of modern art. Bringing the room together. Mike stayed as still as possible as he heard the footsteps grow nearer. He knew the man who chased him was wearing heavy-duty boots. So it seemed. He knew it was him by the voice anyway from he shouted 'OI.'

The man entered the living room, all stern and full of worry why his 'Babe' hadn't been answered. The answer laid before him. James fell to the floor and tried to revive her. 'Loraine, Loraine.' He repeated as he tried to bring her back. CPR and chest compressions did nothing, only gave him hope. He rested his head on her cold chest. Her skin showing through her nighty and he started to cry. Mike peeked from the table. 'Shit, please fuck off.' He whispered. The man pulled out his phone and Mike realised what he was going to do. The cops were the last thing he wanted. He just satisfied his need and now the possibility of never doing it again frightened him. Living with a constant migraine and hatred. Seeing that bitch of a mother every day? Yeah right, he thought. He had to act now!

'Yes, I'd like to report a dead body.' He sniffed up to keep his nose from running. Now was the time, the plan was simple (if it even could be called a plan, more of a quick decision.) knock him out, hang up the call then disappear, oh and don't let him see your face. Mike scooched around the far corner still out of sight. He got himself pumped up reached up from the side of the table and picked up one of the sharpest knives, just in case. He set off with confidence in his strides but as he got closer, he started to panic. 'Yes, the address is- 'He heard Mike's feet tapping on the wood floor as he entered his space. He turned around to see a figure dressed in all black with mud on the bottom of his joggers. Grey Nike air max (almost black from the mud) and an expression which could haunt adults never mind children. He threw his phone and lunged at his attacker, knocking Mike off-balance. He slid across the freshly cleaned floor and ended up banging into the radiator, falling flat on his ass but jumping straight back on to his feet. He was alert, the adrenaline was shooting through his body as heroin would to a smack rat in the town centre.

'You!' he shouted as he threw a fist Mike's way. Perfectly dodged like Tyson in his prime, he sent one back and landing it on the end of his chin. James stumbled and Mike rushed at him and flew through the air with his right leg outright. Hitting James in the gut sending him down in the just been kicked in the nuts position. He hit the ground and his skull crashed hard. Mike jumped on him as he did to his wife but this time there was more of a fight. James got his arms under his and ran them around Mike's, breaking free of his hold. James grabbed his zip and head-butted him hard in the nose. Mike did end up with a busted nose after all. James got up slowly and made his way over. Mike knew he couldn't get caught. Either James had to be silenced or it was life in prison. As he was about to stamp on Mike, he took out the knife from his back pocket and stabbed it right in his Achilles tendon. A huge scream echoed the house. He fell back holding his leg in the air with a knife still in the wound. Mike shot up and turned him over on to his stomach, he never killed a man before and he didn't want to start now. He wrapped his arms around his neck and began to apply pressure. The 'Sleeper' worked a treat for knocking people out. It took a minute and a few seconds, and he eventually drifted off. Mike collapsed in relief, wiping his nose of the blood. He put his sleeve over it to stop any dripping on the floor 'I was never here.'

He scurried into the kitchen to find duct tape or anything to tie that asshole up with. he stopped mid-way through the top drawer and put some kitchen roll up both nostrils. He continued and eventually came across a roll of Sellotape. 'Perfect.' He rushed back in and removed his gloves so he could find the end of the roll, which always annoyed him. He once vowed to create a device that could find the end for you but instead, he chose to kill people. He tied up the man's hands, wrapping it around a good 9 or 10 times, and got ready to make his perfect escape. The 5th had been killed and he managed to restrain the husband as well. He felt invincible. Like he owned the world, no one could stop Mike Ashburn. He stopped giving himself praise when he realised, he made the biggest fuck up a serial killer could make. Worse than leaving evidence behind. He knew he couldn't kill men and he had just given himself the only reason he ever would kill a man.

'This mother fucker has seen my face' Mike's face dropped so hard he nearly heard it thud on the wood. 'Fuck.'

CHAPTER SEVENTEEN:

Ben stood on the corner of Church street which eventually ran into Peel Parade. His house was about a mile away, a long walk when you were intoxicated but he somehow made it every time he walked it. He had checked his phone ten minutes ago, 10:01 PM was the time so it was 10:11 he thought. This was welcomed news. The Jet overnight garage was still open where he could have a pit stop like he always did. A Ginsters chicken and bacon pasty sounded great round about now since he had spewed his guts up in the toilets at the Blacksmith. As soon as he tasted the Vodka Red Bull he knew. He could still feel the sting from his nostrils from when it oozed from his nose as well as his mouth. It became harder and harder to walk, he grew hungry and more tired. He was up at 6 and on the clock at 7. The rain however made it hard to see, a tsunami was hitting the streets with no intention of stopping. The cold droplets kept hitting his pale eyes. He could just about make out the Yellow Jet sign for the Garage, just as he squinted to look at it, his stomach dropped again. Not to vomit but for the other revolting action.

He swung the door open for the men's room and shot into the first available cubical. He finished up, almost vomiting again and exited the cubical. He could hear the running of the far taps of the last sink. The overflow of water trickled down onto the yellow moldy floor. Ben stood for a minute and tried to make the room come around again. A chicken and bacon pasty is needed ASAP. To his astonishment, on the running taps stood just what he wanted. A precious pasty paired with a can of Pepsi. Ben licked his lips. Free food was not to snuffed at, especially in Barnsley as no one did anything for anyone around here. He stumbled forward into the huge puddle the taps had made and reached out for the pre-packed goodness.

'Hello, Ben.' Out came the figure from the last cubical. With her arms around her back and slightly leaning forward she smiled.

'Do I know you?' Ben screwed up his face and stared at her in confusion. He had seen that beautiful face somewhere before. That perfectly made bust, the huge porn star booty and her cherry plump lips were enough to make any man drool. He studied her deeper, miming words as she winked at him. 'Sorry love, You're not my type.' He held his hands up hoping the goddess wouldn't be offended.

'I know, you prefer men, don't you?' she raised her eyebrows and waited for the penny to drop.

'It's you! From the Blacksmith!' he shouted with excitement. Afternoon gameshows where his favourite and always got worked up when he was right. He knew he was right.

Confusion set over him again. 'What do you want?' he asked opening the pasty. Questions can wait, food was a must.

'I won't fuck about with you Ben, I need information which I know you possess.' She said. Her voice was soft on his ears, but he didn't like this. A random woman wanted some information he supposedly possessed. This should be good he thought.

'Ok love, you ask what you want to know, and I'll tell you why I can't tell you.' Trying to be funny never was one of his strong points. It worked on Troy when they went out but that was about it. He leaned on the sink as he finished the last bite of the freebie, then opened the blue Pepsi can.

No wonder you're a fat basted she thought as she watched him gobble away like Shrek when he has the candlelit dinner on his own in first movie. She ignored his clever comment and proceeded.

'I need certain information on a Mr Mike Ashburn.' She paused. 'I know him from a while ago.' She hoped he buy that lame bullshit story.

'Sorry, don't know any Mick Astern.' He said genuinely believing he said his name right. He stumbled slightly as he let out a little chuckle. She didn't look happy with his lie.

'Listen to me, you scratch my back, I'll scratch yours. Trust me you want me on your side.' She stared at Ben hard enough to penetrate his skin. Ben didn't hear as he was gulping down the sugary contents of the can. 'Did it hurt Ben?' she asked. Ben froze

'How do you-.'

'Know your name? I know a lot of things about you, you tubby shit head. I know you like men and your wife left you because she didn't marry a puff. I know you and Troy are good friends and you both work with Mike. I even know what happened to your sister.' She knew she had him now. Right under her thumb.

'Don't you dare!' Ben screamed at her. She replied with 'Did it hurt then? When you killed her? When you suffocated her with your huge back? How old was she?' Ben had slid down the wall and tears filled his face. The pain was unbearable. Having the guilt of rolling over that when he babysat for his new-born sister at just 14 years of age. Weighing a whopping 17 stone 7 pounds. He was obese but that didn't mean he was a bad person. However, his parents disowned him when they returned home from the theatre. Watching a play of 'Romeo & Juliet, his father loved the classics and his mother bared them. They returned to see their obese son starfishing on his bed to be woken up with the question 'Where's your Sister?' his Sister Rose was just 6 weeks old when she passed, and Ben was just 14 when he was kicked out. It was investigated but the judge ruled it to be a genuine accident and didn't charge him with manslaughter. How could someone kill another in their sleep? Not on purpose anyway.

'how, how do you know that?' he managed to stutter through the tears.

'Rose was her name, right?' she asked. He nodded.

'Hey, it was an accident, Look I need to know where he lives.' She waited for him to man up. He wiped his flat face and sniffled like he had the flu. 'Fuck, you!' he said in an almost evil voice. Similar to the voice of Bane from The Dark Knight Rises. His new friend bent down to meet his eye line. Revealing her bust from her blouse. Ben stole a peek, he was drunk and even though he was gay, he still liked breasts. When he was drunk, he liked anything, he must have been BI.

'Last chance.' She explained. Her eyes darting at each one of his tearful ones. He leaned forward on the wet floor and was about to tell her where she could stick it. Who the hell did she think she was, demanding info on Mike and bringing up his dead sister? How dare she, but she dared. As he thought of saying all that ran threw his head, her right knee connected with his nose and shattered it into pieces. Like glass. He let out a huge 'AAAAGHHH' which came from deep inside of him. She stepped back and kicked him, this time in his torso knocking the wind out of him. He was a big man, who could take a blow or two, but she was strong and nimble. Like a TI-CHI master.

'Address.' She said in a firm tone. Ben sat there in the pools gasping for air. He held his arm up in the air pointing a finger to the sky which said one minute. His tongue hung from his mouth, dry from the gasps of breath, it had turned almost a greyish colour. He caught his breath eventually. His size made it hard to breathe over the fat which surrounded his organs. Not as hard it was for Rose to breathe that dreadful night. 'I don't know who you-' She cut his lame excuse short and punched him in his throat. He copied the gasp from the first blow and took even longer to talk this time.

'You scratch my back, I scratch yours.' He looked puzzled as he stared deep into her swamp green eyes.

'Come on Ben, I can help you.' She explained

'Help me how?' he managed to say in his breathe. He had no idea what he needed help with. he had everything he had ever wanted except a family. A lot like his colleague Mike, he too came from a broken home. Only he didn't know it.

'Your parents, I could give you their address in exchange for Mike's.' she had hope in her voice knowing that would do the trick.

'You know where they are?' He asked. He stood up and tried not to look embarrassed, the alcohol had worn off and he was more in the moment. That kicking had brought him back around. She glanced at him and pulled out a cigarette. She offered him one and he accepted. They both lit up and inhaled almost in sync.

'I do. I can tell you and I promise I will, as soon as I have what I want.' She was in control. Ben knew he couldn't take her on, he couldn't move quick enough.

'Stone Brooke House, Regent Street in the town centre, apartment 49.' Ben felt instant guilt about giving away private information on who he considered a dear friend. But he needed to make amends with his family. It had been 31 years since he last saw them. Surely they missed him he hoped.

'Thank you, Ben, see that wasn't hard was. Now, before I tell you where they are, I need you to do one last thing for me.' She waited for his reply.

'For fuck sake, what?' he couldn't wait he needed to know now! He didn't trust her, but she knew all about him, there was honor in the exchange, so he thought.

'Say hello to your sister for me.'

CHAPTER EIGHTEEN:

Marley licked Emily's face instantly waking her up. She had been fast asleep for most of ten minutes, but it turns out it was 30 minutes. 10:23 PM and Mike still wasn't back. He had called her at 6 PM asking for a favour. A long walk with Marley and to watch his flat until he returned home so he could pay her was easily worth the 40 pounds he had offered. She was a huge dog lover, so this wasn't considered work to her. Emily Wilde was 22 years old. She was blonde and gorgeous which always helped in life's everyday situations. Like the time she forgot her card at Asda and the nice guy on the till let her off. The bill was only £3.40 but she thought it was better than nothing, right? She stood up, pulling her leggings back up from where they had drooped down while she had tossed and turned on the sofa, and stretched so hard she went all dizzy and fuzzy. She reached for her phone on the coffee table while still petting the happy pooch with the other hand. She had 2 missed calls from Elizabeth. 'Liz' was her very proud girlfriend of 6 months, but deep down Emily was becoming exhausted with her. Every meeting the pair had was becoming more draining. Liz was full of life, while Emily wasn't. She was a photographer for the Barnsley Echo, which was a well-paid job, however, it was also an easy job for her. She had learned to point a camera by the age of 2. She was born for it. Liz used to always praise her photo's, forever saying she could photograph their wedding which would never happen. She put her phone back in her pocket.

'I can't be assed with her Marls.' She walked to the patio and let him out for a piss while sniffing a key of white powder from a little baggie. It instantly brought her out of the after nap stage and she could take him out again if she wanted to. She gurned and made some weird looking faces as the Coke hit her hard. Taking her to euphoria. Mike's best friend eventually came back inside, drenched from the rain. She proceeded to dry him, so he didn't get cold. The Springer had a human-like smile on his face and an uncontrollable waggy tail. She collected her things, put her phone on silent and began to wish him goodbye. If she hurried, she could still make the 10:31 PM bus back to Shafton, which conveniently dropped her outside her shared house. She enjoyed Mike's late nights, she always caught up on her sleep. Living there was ok to begin with, but it got more crowded over time. Less room in the living room, more labeled food was starting to go missing and at the end of January just gone the rent money had gone missing from her housemate Joel's room. They all knew Emily enjoyed the powder, so she was the number one suspect. Even though she was innocent they deem her guilty.

She swung the door open and slammed it shut, alerting everyone she was leaving (mostly in a rush) she started making her way to the end of the hall when apartment 3 opened. Emily clapped eyes on the young woman standing in the doorway, posing as if she was a model on the catwalk. She was fully dressed, still in a 'Pierce the Veil' T-shirt and Blue denim jeans. White Chuck Taylor's and a few piercings which automatically meant she liked that bang-bang music.

'Hey, Em.' She smiled and looked deep into her huge pupils.

'Oh, hey Amy, how's things?' She asked keeping her head down. Trying to hide the fact she was as high as a kite. The Cuban cut she had was some strong stuff. The strongest she had in a while.

'I'm good cheers, you walking to the station?'

'Uh-huh, my bus comes at half ten, but I think I'll miss it.' She looked at Amy and studied her. She had missed her pristine figure and her bubbly personality. She never meant to end their relationship so soon, she didn't allow it to blossom into something wonderful.

'Want me to walk you?' she fluttered her eyes hoping she would say yes.

'Nah, that's okay, you don't have to do that.' She explained. Holding her lips firm together.

'You are aware that there is a serial killer in Barnsley, right?' She asked, genuinely concerned if she had been living under a rock.

'Oh, fuck yeah, how many bodies?' She asked in shock.

'4 in 3 months.' She said with wide eyes. 'You want to be getting a taxi home, fuck the bus.' Amy didn't dare invite her in like she wanted to. She still had feelings for her ex, but she didn't know how to tell her. They had only dated for 3 months last year. April to July was the best time she had ever had.

'want to come in and order one?' Amy waited anxiously.

'That's probably the best thing to do.' She chuckled as she walked towards Amy's door. She stood aside and let her. Shutting the door cautiously and smiling behind her back. Emily felt at home right away. Spending most of their time together in Amy's bedroom. The place hadn't changed much she thought. Except for a few new pictures on her walls. Mostly of a new face, Emily had never seen before. Hugging and posing with Amy.

'New bird?' she asked. Intrigued.

'Oh, yeah that's Stacey. Been seeing her around a month now.' She sounded a little edge as she said it.

'A month? Must be the one to be hanging from your wall, right?' Emily walked straight through the hall and into the living area, a lot like Mike's apartment but this one had a little more space. She sat at the table next to the window, the one she used to have coffee at when she stopped over.

'Would you like anything, beer, coffee?' Asked Amy standing by the fridge, just a few yards away from her. Emily knew she should probably get on home, but she wanted to stay. She didn't want to be in the company of Liz. She didn't have the energy for her overactive compliments and her bubbly personality.

'Coffee would be nice.' She said, fluttering her eyelashes just like Amy had at the door. She put the kettle on and started to think of small talk. Amy made her way over and sat opposite.

'Can you remember Cannon Hall?' she asked with a smile.

'OH MY GOD!' she laughed with saliva flying out from inside her teeth. 'When I fell flat on my ass trying to feed that stupid goat?' hysterical laughter filled the apartment by the pair of them. Emily laid flat on the table with her head on the surface and her arms stretched outright, still laughing. Emily caressed her pale hands, with such charisma. Almost worshiping them. Emily looked up and met her eye line. They both just went away for a while. Touching, reminiscing and being with each other once again. Emily could feel happiness make its way through her heart, love, and affection filling her up like candy in a piñata. Amy fluttered her eyes once again and said, 'Do you remember what my bedroom looks like?' Emily gulped and followed her lead into her bedroom. She didn't feel bad for cheating on Liz. As far as she was aware Liz could be getting murdered by the 'Snapper' and she wouldn't give a fuck. At this moment all she cared about was Amy's cherry lips and her magical way of making her feel fuzzy. One thing did play on her mind though, she never enjoyed dumping people and she knew she had to do it tomorrow morning. Tomorrow morning for sure.

CHAPTER NINETEEN:

James had been tied up for 20 minutes. To Mike, it felt like a lifetime. His nose had finally stopped gushing blood, but there was a bigger problem at large. He had a dead body and a live body in the same room. James had seen his face. He had skin samples under his fingernails probably. Tonight had been such a wonderful night, but now it could be the end of his reign. The end of an era he thought. He had only one option and that was to silence him. Permanently. But how? He knew he couldn't. He only killed so he wouldn't go insane from the issues that bitch had infected him with. Such a great coping mechanism. He felt no urge to kill a man. Except for Troy when he was being a prick. But he would never follow through on it. Or would he? He ran his hand through his hair as he thought hard on the situation. The man was out of it. He has a knife sticking out of his ankle and his wife is dead at the side of him. 'Fuck.' He paced up and down. Wearing out the wooden floor and to his surprise, the man began to moan in pain. Mike stopped dead in his tracks and examined him. He was a well-built man, your average gym-goer. Huge tree trunk arms and legs. Mike felt proud he had managed to restrain such a beast.

'You…...cunt!' struggled the croaky voice. His leg had gone pale. A pool had formed on the wooden floor from the wound. Mike didn't respond, he didn't know how to. 'It's you, you're the Snapper.' He said. Worry set on Mike's face. He knew he had to silence him.

'Congratulations, you know someone famous.' He said trying to humour him.

'FUCK YOU!' he screamed followed by an outburst of pain. Mike walked over to him and hovered. Gently in the air.

'I am the so-called Snapper. And you are going to be my first male victim.' He said unconvincingly. James didn't listen though, he was squirming on the floor form the pain. Mike didn't even know if what he said was true. Only time would tell.

Mike studied Loraine's corpse laying on the wooden floor. Her eyes wide and her neck bruised. He felt proud, almost too proud. 'She's dead James. Nothing you can do I'm afraid. She was my fifth.' He walked over to her and looked down. 'She'll always be precious to me.' James's eyes widened in disbelief that he was in the presence of a serial killer. Not just your average nutter, a man who has killed 5 women in 3 months and not been caught. No leads on him existed. The only evidence there was is James. He knew his secret, and this fact scared him half to death.

'What are you going to do with me?' He asked holding his leg in the air.

'Me, me, me. That's all it is with you, isn't it? I've just told you that your wife is dead, and all your asking is what's going to happen to you. That's how I knew you'd care too much about that horrible car.' Said Mike as James's eye's filled with tears. The realisation was too much, and he let his leg go from his hands and covered his face as he started to grieve.

'If you must know, I haven't decided yet.' Said Mike staring at the knife poking out of James's ankle. James's tears came to a slow holt and he stared at the ceiling. He was in a bad situation and he knew it. He had heard of the Snapper in the news and how ruthless he was, but James had always imagined him a little more...... menacing. This guy was just your average looking Joe. He looked more like a junky than a killer. His lean physique and his scruffy bristly black beard made him look a little worn. If James could walk, he knew he could take him. The first round didn't count he thought. He had just discovered his wife dead, so he wasn't on his full game. He was surprised though, why would a serial killer of his reputation leave his assumed next victim with a weapon? All he had to was pluck up the courage to pull the knife out, then he had the upper hand. His hands were tied but he could reach the handle of the devil's kitchen knife. If he pulled it out though there was a danger of him bleeding out. Maybe that's what the 'Snapper' wanted. His only option was to absorb all the pain and go in for the second round.

Mike looked around the room and assessed his surroundings. He saw what he presumed to be a male's dressing gown. The Navy Blue reminded him of the Navy. Almost like a black. 'That's it.' Mike's face had grown a huge smile. Seeing the long piece of belt for the robe had sent him a brainwave. He quickly turned around and laid the soul of his shoe on James' face. Knocking him out cold. His brilliant idea would prove everyone wrong who had ever called him 'stupid.' Throwing the police off-track would be great for his anxiety. All he needed was some rope and a pen and paper and the 'Snapper' would be gone. He would have killed his wife in a blind rage, left a note with his reasons for his death and his killing spree and hung himself from the banister in the hallway. It was perfect. The perfect way to get away with murder.

The Summer sun beat down on the back of Mike's neck as he and his father walked through the canal's dirt path. Dragging his fishing box (which was also his chair for the day) through the foliage and the sea of litter, his dad stumbled over a root. Dave Ashburn was ready for this day with his son. Getting away from the butchers' shop was good for him and getting away from his horrible wife was good for Mike. 'Stupid root' he said as he looked back at the hazard. He glanced at his son to see the look of excitement on his face. I need to do this more, get him out of her way he thought. He smiled and Mike smiled back. Both eager for the first cast they walked to their favourite spot.

A little podium made of new wood was in a prime spot for Perch and even a couple of Carp

(So other fishermen had claimed.) Mike put his fishing box at the left of the podium and his father set his down to the right. Mike pulled the cover off his second-hand rod his father had got him from a loyal customer for a steal. He didn't like it that much, but it did the job of letting him fish by himself, without having to share his dads. It was the middle of October and it was a cold one. The wind howled through the trees in Carlton causing quite the upset in the town. Mainly to the elderly. Mike knew Christmas wasn't too far away and he knew exactly what he was going to ask Santa for. A brand new Anglers fishing pole. An hour in and neither of them had had a nibble. Mike was hoping his father wouldn't get bored and hurry them back to his mother. Mike loved just been out on the canal. Even if it was windy and they didn't catch anything. He loved being in the fresh air of planet earth. Less chance of been carted off to the chamber.

'Dad?'

'Yes son?' said Dave. Still looking at the clear water of the pond. Seeing little insects flying around the surface and little tadpoles swaying through oxygen bubbles.

'Why does Mummy hate me?' Asked Mike.

'She doesn't hate you, son, she loves you with all her heart.' He explained to his confused son. 'Look the reason she puts you in that cupboard is to make sure you are out of the way when…'

'You fight?' Mike said finishing his sentence. He wasn't dumb, he knew what went on when he was locked up. Mainly because the old house had paper-thin walls.

'Yes son, it's to make sure you are protected. So we don't hurt your precious soul. You're such a lovely child, we don't want to expose you to so much negative energy when we disagree. Does that make sense?' his father waited eagerly for a reply.

'Why don't you and Mummy just get along then?' Was Mike's reply.

CHAPTER TWENTY:

Jack was just in the middle of a dream about the woman he nearly bagged at the Blacksmith when his phone pinged. The time was 11:47 PM. The message read SNAPPER VICTIM, ROYSTON JET GARAGE. The number was unknown, he tried to dial it, but it went straight to voicemail. Who on earth would text him such a thing? Was someone messing with him? Taunting him that he didn't have a lead? All he knew is that he couldn't let it go until he had seen it for himself. He thought it would be best to go alone. If it was just a hoax it was better to waste his own time than the time of South Yorkshire police. Resources were tight as it is without a detective wasting their time as well. He shot out of bed and got dressed. A casual T-shirt and jogging bottoms with a navy blue Jumper would be casual enough. He had just dropped off when the message had come through. He was used to no sleep lately anyway. Might as well be investing his time wisely, maybe actually getting somewhere with the 'Snapper' case. He knew he was over the limit, but he didn't care. Nothing a Mickey D's coffee couldn't sort out.

He arrived at the Petrol station just before midnight. His Coffee was steaming hot, the queue at Mickey D's had been fairly short (to his surprise.) he hadn't let anyone know where he was or what he was doing. But in the end who even cared?

Certainly not his wife. His boss just wanted results rather than updates of his movements and the public wanted this sonofabitch caught. He had parked in the closest parking space available to the Shop area of the station and finally switched off the ignition. The shop was a brand of its own he thought named Carlton's Convenience. The kids had nicknamed it CARCON for short. He got out of his car after he put the 'ON DUTY/CALL' sign on the dashboard. He was met by cold rain once again shattering the spirits of Barnsley. Jack looked around as he got drenched. He never minded the rain, but he didn't like it either. If he had to be wet to do his job, so be it. After all, his job was all he had. He managed to make out the inside of the shop and the spotty teenager working behind the till. There wasn't much around the Garage. Just a long road in and out of Royston. Like a road on Route 66. Jack knew the place to check was the toilets. A perfect place for illegal activity. No cameras and secluded cubicles, who wouldn't commit any crime there?

He jogged through the opening which the rain had control of and arrived at the door of the women's toilet. He pulled out his trusty torch, which he had since his first year on the job (now 11 years on the force) and edged around the corner. Entering the smelly toilets he couldn't help but remember the Birmingham case. That's where he learned to check the bathroom. Always try to check those first before anywhere else. When he entered the Toilets in Cineworld in Birmingham town centre. He found the notorious Mario Russo in the middle of one of his kill cycles. Originally born in Milan in 1986, The 'Setto' killer (Italian for septum) was about to rip the septum out of his 8th victim before Jack wrestled him to the ground and saved the victims' life. He got away with a slight deformity to his nose. Instead of slashing open his guts then removing his septum as his trophy. He decided to do this kill back to front. From then on, he always checked the toilets. Priority.

The Ladies room was empty, except a rat scurrying along the pale pink tiles. He pulled his phone out and read the message again. It defiantly meant this garage as this was the only one remotely close to Royston. He shone his torch around the dead cubicles and the dark corners to reveal nothing. He walked out back into the rain and headed to the Men's. he noticed the Geeky looking Checkout boy staring at him. I'll question him after he thought. He reached the door and could immediately smell the ammonia reeking from the drains. He turned his torch back on and shone it through the thick shadows. The cubicles were empty. The far sink was full and over spilling onto the pale blue tiles. The lights didn't work as Jack had found the switched and tried to flick them on. His torch was up to the role and lit it up the best it could. He entered the toilets, cautiously. Slowly edging along the gritty tiles. Almost shuffling. He held his torch in his right hand picked up a swollen plank of wood with his left. (swollen from the rain just sprinkling in from the doorway.) He stopped and listened for any sign of the stench pit being inhabited. Nothing. He carried on a few seconds before a loud groan came from the last cubicle. Jack froze and held the plank tighter. Hoping a firmer grip would mean he could swing and hit harder. The groan became more frequent and louder, he hoped he hadn't heard him walking to his vicinity. (definitely a male due to the deepness of the groan.) He stood a still as he could just outside the last cubicle door. He wished he had stayed home, he didn't like to admit to himself, but he felt a little…. scared. for the first time in a long time. He took a deep breath and placed his sweaty palm on the door. Another groan was almost in sync with his touch. He steadied the door as it creaked open to reveal a middle-aged man sat on the toilet with blood all over his face. His arms were badly bruised, and his legs were broken. On his right hand, he had a broken ring finger. The man was drifting in and out of consciousness as he could just make out a man stood before him.

'Oh my god...' Stuttered jack in disbelief. Was this the first live victim of the 'Snapper?' had this man seen his face? Too many questions flooded Jack's brain. The possibility that he could get somewhere on this case dawned on him. He rushed into the cubicle and checked the man's face to see where the bleeding had spewed from. The victim had a large cut on his forehead. Stretching four inches. An easy fix with stitches he thought. He pulled his phone out and dialed 999. He looked at the man to see his eyes were open. He was hanging on. 'What's your name, sir? I'm going to get you help don't worry, you're in good hands. Yes, ambulance, it's DCI Jack brown, I need the full works, possible 'Snapper' victim, alive, servilely injured. Royston Jet Garage. HURRY!'

He hung up and took Ben's hand 'It's okay mate, you're in good hands now. Help is on the way.' Jack noticed the man was trying to say something. The blood on his lips was bubbling as his mouth barely opened. Jack got closer and listened for anything he was trying to say. 'Go on mate, I'm all ears.'

'Wrong…. finger'

Jack glanced at his hands and noticed the wrong finger was stuck up in the air. Broken clean in two.

As the ambulance had arrived and took Ben away to A&E, Jack had the job of interviewing the spotty teenager about a bad assault, currently ruling out attempted murder even though all the signs of the 'Snapper' were there. So he thought.

'Name?' Asked Jack. He was in no mood to piss about, he had to get to the victim and find out as much as possible on his attacker. Then it was all systems go, who knew, new evidence and a new victim could be just the thing he needed to crack the case.

'Ryan Hartwell.' He replied, itching his greasy mop. His face was like a dot to dot puzzle and Jack could tell he would stink, even though he hadn't had a whiff of his aroma yet. His Yellow Jet uniform looked a little discoloured as well as if it hadn't been washed. Just left to collect dust and mold on a chair. 'I'm 21 Years old born on the 2nd of May 1998. I live at 332 Meadow Lane in Goldthorpe and I have never seen that man before in my life.' He said to Jack's surprise. The first time a witness or anyone involved (possibly) had given everything he needed without him asking.

'Somewhere to be Ryan?'

'What do you mean?' he asked, puzzled.

'Well, you're in some hurry to tell me all that aren't you?' Jack closed his pocketbook after jotting all the details down.

'No, but you are. You need to get to that guy and find out who did this. If it was that 'Snapper' you kill the son of a bitch!' Ryan's eyes had fuelled anger behind them as he said that.

Pure rage. Jack paused and waited for him to explain himself as to why he was so angry.

'I'm sorry detective. It's just…. my sister Lauren was taken by him.' Tears had filled his eyes and began to fall, crashing on the laminate floor of the overpriced shop.

'I'm so sorry for your loss.' Jack said, almost whispering. 'But I need to know, did you see anything?' Jack's question hung in the air like Ryan's bad smell. He had a few whiffs during this short conversation. Jack was almost praying this kid had got a good look at him.

'Sorry man, not a thing.' He sniffed 'But we have CCTV covering all angles of the premises. The only problem is there in the back office, the monitors, and they don't trust me with a key yet. Think I might nick something then erase the tape.' He sniffed up again. Looking almost doubtful in his explanation.

'Show me, now.' Demanded Jack. The young adult turned and faced the cigarette counter and began to walk through to the back rooms. Jack followed but this time not as cautious as he was entering the gents. A few twists and turns through a surprisingly big hallway and stepping over unopened stock, they arrived at a room that had a plate on it which read PRIVATE. Jack grabbed the handle and pushed the door open. To Ryan's surprise, it wasn't locked.

'They always keep it locked.' He uttered.

'It was locked.' Jack stepped into the room and saw all of the monitors were static and some had a commercial grey background with a colour strip along the bottom, bellowing out that high pitched screeching noise.

'Someone has kicked it in and destroyed the evidence they were ever here.' Jack was becoming frustrated. One thing after the other. Hopefully, the victim knew how to remember the face. If not. Back to square one.

'It's okay, they keep a USB in the back of that tower that automatically copies anything it records.' Ryan was almost too excited by his helping hand. Jack was a little concerned.

'Can I take it?' Jack knew he was taking it anyway, but he thought he'd be polite.

'Uh- I don't think so- '

'I could arrest you here and now for obstructing an investigation or you could let me take it and pretend the twat who did this took it, and no one would be any the wiser. Don't you want justice for Lauren?' Jack's question once again hung in the air.

'Take it.' Snapped Ryan. Jack walked to the tower and unplugged the 64GB USB stick and put it in his right-hand pocket of the navy blue jumper. He nodded at Ryan and walked back to the front of the shop. He opened the door and ran to his car. The night sky still pissing rain. He jumped in his car as quick as he could. He didn't care if Ryan was lying, he didn't even doubt his statement he had given. All he cared about were what was on this drive and if the Man in A&E had a lead for him.

CHAPTER TWENTY ONE:

Mike was rummaging through the kitchen draws when he heard James make a painful groan for help. He steadied himself and listened. He was back out of it, he hoped. The top drawer of the kitchen had produced Mike with an A4 notepad. Just the thing for a suicide note. He emptied his pockets as his keys and his phone was beginning to irritate him as he was speeding and moving so fast everywhere. The kitchen hadn't produced a pen for him to jot this painful goodbye down. He didn't remember seeing one in the living room or the dining room, so it was finally time to check upstairs. He walked to the front door and locked it with the keys which were hung just in reach (just in case) Mike was surprised no one had come over. Two struggles and a murder and not a neighbour in sight. Some community.

He passed the pictures the dead woman had heard smash and he peeked around the corner to see both husband and wife lifeless.

He began to walk upstairs when one of the stairs creaked and made him jump al little. Just the old fishing podium did when he and his dad went fishing. He erased the thought and thought of the matter at hand. Framing a man for this murder. These murders. He reached the top of the landing, not even noticing all the family photos on the wall on the way up. He was faced with three doors. To say it was a big house there weren't too many rooms. Must have huge space inside he thought. Door number one revealed the bathroom. Completely spotless of any mould or dirt, sparkling. Behind door number two was the master bedroom. A little too plain for a married couple. A dull colour of grey had the basics inside, just the bed, wardrobes and an impressive huge TV. At least 55 inch hanging on the far wall. Door number three had some colourful drawings on the outside which made Mike have a sudden realisation. The phot he smashed of the little boy. He stared at the door and there it was. A big four letting sign hanging from a nail in the wood, supported by Spider-man and Captain America was the word JAKE in big colourful letters. Oranges and Blue's mainly. 'Fuck.' He said under his breath. So he had a bigger problem on his hands. What is going to happen to this kid? Could he take both this innocent child's parents? He didn't think he could, but he had no choice. This kid would be better off dead than without his parents. Mike had first-hand experience of this nature and it wasn't pleasant.

'No witnesses.' He said to himself as he grasped the handle, gently opening the door and sliding inside the bedroom which was lit up by a night light.

CHAPTER TWENTY-TWO:

Mike stood there, peacefully as the small child was sound asleep. Dreaming dreams of his favourite things. The sight of the child sent him back to all the times he had dreamed of an amazing life, laughing and living in perfect harmony with his parents. If only if only. Instead, he went through a life of misery. Mainly accompanied by loneliness. He had his trusty sidekick Marley but sometimes he wishes he had someone to talk to, someone to confide in. He hadn't seen his mother since she killed his dad. He believed the last day he saw her she buried him in the garden, but he was lumbered into care before he knew it. Returning to his old property to find a new porch sitting area had been built over the possible spot. Somethings would never be answered. Like is his father alive? Or, why does Mike feel the need to kill people? He'll never know.

The child hadn't moved a muscle since his arrival in his bedroom. Mike stared at him, not moving, not blinking just staring. Jake let out a deep breath from nowhere, bringing Mike back to earth. He snapped out of it, his deep trance of another fishing trip and started to edge towards him, just hovering above his set of draws next to his bed. He looked down to see a really cute looking kid. Freckles and his brown hair highlighted his chubby little cheeks. eyes shut tight, he was dead to the world. Mike felt sadness creep along his troubled soul. He couldn't feel anger or worry, just pain. Pain of an unloved child. A robbed child. Robbed of his innocence and forced to grow up and exploited to horror at such a young age. A tear formed on the lashes of his left eye and he wiped it away as quickly as possible. He took another look at Jake and slowly headed for the door. Been as quiet as he could. Doing his best not to make any sound. He noticed a desk and suddenly remembered what he came upstairs for. There it was sat on itself in an old cup. An old cup which he presumed were for writing utensils. His ticket to freedom would be wrote in black ink.

Jack had arrived home 30 minutes later after interviewing the attendant. He would have been home sooner, but he stopped off for another Mickey D's delicious slow-roasted blend of coffee. He was up so he might as well stay up he thought. 'Who knows, might get somewhere tonight.'

He was sat in his usual spot on the left-hand side of his worn-out sofa. His dog Max fast on at the side of him. His laptop was just booting up and his coffee sat on the armrest. His screensaver lit to display his daughters' adorable smile. He sighed. But no time for being sad. He pulled out the USB drive from his jumper and plugged it in just before typing in his passcode to access the home screen. The bottom left corner alerted him that a new device had been inserted, he clicked on it bringing up all the storage for that device. A file read 'CCTV' he clicked it and watched the screen display four screens labeled one- four. The first box was covering the men's room. The second was covering the women's room. The third was covering the shop floor and he could see Ryan walking up an isle with a mop and bucket. The fourth was covering the outside area where people fill up their vehicles. Jack hovered over the first box, the men's room and a little bar for the minutes popped up, he scrolled along to the time 7:57 PM. Not a single thing had changed from the image. He scratched his head and took a sip of his warm coffee. He hovered over the second camera and set it to the same time. Nothing but an old woman coming out of the women's room. 'Too old to be a killer.' He said to his dog Max. Max replied with a heavy breath. He set the other two to the same time and came up with nothing. He skipped to 10 PM and instantly hit the jackpot. 'I was due some luck.' He said. On camera three he caught the back of what looked like a female, hood up. Black jeans and black boots. Her sweatshirt was also black. She reminded him of Black cat form Spider-Man. She was just lurking in the isle's picking things up but not examining them. Doing this several times until the time 10:02 when she turned her head and headed out of the store. She held her head down and more or less skipped to the men's room. Heading inside the door. A few seconds had passed until Ben appeared on camera four stumbling through the tumbling rain. Jack sat back in disbelief to how easy he had come across some fresh evidence. Had he just seen the Snapper on tape? Maybe. He hit rewind on the main control panel and all four skipped back. He froze the image and he could see her blurred face. Old and wrinkled. He copied the file to a separate document to make sure he had it safe. Finally a little luck. In a few hours, he would go to the station and check with Sarah what Sally Ashburn used to look like. But first, a visit to the hospital.

CHAPTER TWENTY-THREE:

To whom discovers this letter:

My name is James Watson and I am the one they call the 'Snapper.'

My wife Loraine was strangled by me, after figuring out the truth. I couldn't let her live on with the guilt of my actions so I decide she, the love of my life would be my fifth and final victim. My son Jake will awake without any parents but it is for the best. My need to kill has taken me down a dark path and I have lost everything I have ever cared about. I can't control what lurks beneath the surface. My need to kill can't continue to take beloved mothers from their children and loving families. This is my way of gaining control once again. To the people of Barnsley and the victims' families, I am truly sorry. I don't expect or want your forgiveness, I don't deserve it. But I feel the world deserves to know the truth to who committed such unspeakable evil acts. Please don't take my son into care, please send him to a relative. Just because his father is a maniac doesn't mean he is an evil kid. Please don't hide the truth from him. The quicker he knows the quicker he can heal and hopefully live a normal life. Once again, I'm sorry and what needs to be done, is done.

James.

'Like fuck they will ever buy that!' James said with laughter. Mike folded the letter up and rested it neatly in his pocket. 'You talk as if I'm dead. You don't have the fucking balls to fucking kill me!' He screamed. Spraying the floor with his spittle. Mike hovered for a minute, almost in different dimensions.

'Your son will get up tomorrow and discover you hanging from the bannister. I am sorry. But I need a fresh start, to clear my name.' said Mike. Piercing James's eyes with the sternest of looks.

'I-I.' James couldn't speak. His time was up.

'I'm going to check your garage for any rope, or you could tell me where it is and save me time.' Before James could answer Mike said. 'Didn't think so, you try anything, and I swear to you, your son will hang with you, understand?' James nodded not making a sound. Not even a murmur of 'Uh-uh.' James stayed as still as possible truly terrified as Mike walked past him. He reached the back patio door behind the table in the dining room and stepped out into the garden, the same garden just a few hours ago he selected Loraine for tonight. So far so good. Since he had killed her his head hadn't made a single bolt of pain. He felt revived, he believed he truly had found his pain killer. If he managed to pull this off, he had to stop snapping fingers. He could live with that. He walked over the clean flags, the rain had stopped which made him feel a little sad, but it would surely return. He reached the garage and opened the side door. As he entered he was greeted by a cobweb straight across the face. 'Nice.' He said as he searched for the light switch. He flicked it and illuminated the depressed-looking garage. Hardly anything was on show, just a few tools, and a chest freezer. Guessing that was where they kept the meat and frozen veg. luckily James was also a fisherman like Mike. And hanging from the roof and the beams, which ran horizontal, was his fishing tackle. A lot like Mike's gear, A fishing box/seat, big enough and strong enough to hold a forty-pound man. A few rods and poles and a large landing net for when he caught anything. Holding it all together in place on the roof was a spider's web of blue rope. The same roll he saw at the builder's merchants when he bought his spray paint. 'Need to cut it down.' He said to himself.

'Hello, Mike.' A voice said from behind him. Echoing through the heavy-duty walls. He spun around fast enough to pull his neck and send a shock of pain through his spine. He was met with the same expression he had on his face.

'Who are you?' He asked in disbelief. Mike stood before himself, like looking in a mirror or it could have even been his long lost twin.

'I'm you Mike, deep down inside you are dying from all this. It's tearing you apart!' He sounded genuinely concerned with his actions.

'What makes you the expert huh?' He replied. Not knowing what to say. He started to become nervous about the fact he was staring at himself. 'The world can't have two of me can it?'

'I'm your conscience you mentally ill prick! Look at what you're doing! Killing an innocent man, robbing that young boy of his only parent since you fucking killed the other one! Such a fucking waste of flesh!' Tears began to form in his ducts. Such a gut punch.

I…. I have to- '

'No! you, Mike Ashburn, want to. You want to kill that man because killing is your coping mechanism, isn't it? A way to get back at her right?' Mike felt sick as he was hearing the truth from someone else's mouth for the first time.

'Like she's watching all of this and she'll coming running to you apologising for what she did, right?' He had his arms held out waiting for Mike to respond. Silence. 'You know she'll never come. She didn't care about you then, why would she care now? Why would she even want to see you?' She even killed your dad Mi- '

Mike swung his arms through the air screaming 'SHUT UP!' at the top of his lungs. His face bright red, he smashed his hand into the wall. He was helicoptering his arms almost like he was seeing Slipknot for the first time and he was loving it. He finally stopped and checked to see if he had gone. To his relief, he was once again alone. He lent up against the east wall and slid down it, painting his back with dust. He had his knees up to his stomach and rested his arms in front of his face. He began to cry. Not thinking about anything, just letting the realisation of the knock-on effect of his actions would have. He just sat there and let it all wash him in pain and evil. He knew it was all wrong and he had a place reserved in hell. As he was crying his eyes out, like a student being severely bullied in school. He asked himself 'Why does it feel so good?'

CHAPTER TWENTY-FOUR:

Mike had cut down the fishing tackle and let it crash on the cold concrete floor. He pulled the rope through a maze of holes in the steel beams and wrapped it around his arm and his thumb, forming a perfect hoop. He grabbed one end and made a traditional executioner knot. He had learned how to make from a young age, his interest in death had always been around. He wiped his eyes, the tears had subsided for a while but there was still a little emotion left behind in lashes of his eyes. His feelings had come to the surface and he didn't like it. Seeing himself telling him the truth of the matter was almost heartbreaking. What he was doing was not human. He knew he deserved to be the one who dies but…. He just couldn't bring himself to own up to his actions. He had unfinished business anyway. When he had tied these loose ends up he had one goal. Find and kill his mother.

Jack arrived at Barnsley hospital almost excited. For the first time on this case, he had information, which could turn out into a lead if this potential Snapper victim had a good look at the suspect. Jack was sure it was a man, but he had been wrong before. The killer had also mixed up the cycle and gone for a male victim. So far there had been four female victims and now a male victim had survived the attack. Maybe this is why she stuck to women because the men were too strong. All he knew was he needed answers. Fast. The time was 11:37 PM when he asked the receptionist where the possible

Snapper victim was and flashed her his badge. Second floor, ward 35 was where he headed after he got two coffees from the Costa machine outside the WHSmith's.

He walked through the big swinging double doors and flashed his badge once again. They exchanged information on the Victim. 'His name is Ben Hanson, two broken legs, badly bruised in the torso area, broken ring finger on the right hand and a black eye. He'll recover but his legs are in bad shape.' The receptionist glanced down at her desk through her thick jam jar glasses picked up a file and said 'Room seven, he may be asleep, but you can go in.' he nodded at her and walked off. Room seven wasn't admitting any light into the hallway which suggested he was, in fact, asleep but to Jack's surprise, he was awake. He introduced himself as 'DCI Jack Brown South Yorkshire police, may I have a seat, Ben?'

'Only if one of those coffees are for me.' He said in his rich Barnsley accent. Jack studied him for a bit. Both his legs in casts. His black eye was a deep colour of purple. His legs were hanging in the air by swings, just as he had expected. Jack felt sorry for the poor man. 'How old are you sir? If you don't mind me asking.' He asked.

'Young enough to fight that bitch off.' He said, itching his face with his right hand, flashing his broken finger.

'So it was a she then?' Jack took a sip of his coffee to calm his nerves. He must have had a good look. Result he thought. He handed Ben one of the cups.

'OH ARE! Reyt ugly bitch, older than me, but fuck she can feyt. Look at the state of me.' Ben looked a little embarrassed he had his ass kicked by an older woman, but at least he was still alive. Jack pulled out his phone and pulled up a picture he took from his laptop of a close up of the woman from the footage in the shop. 'is this her Ben?'

'THAT'S HER! How did you get that?'

'I've checked the footage and she entered the toilets moments before you did.' Said Jack. Sending a look of worry to him. 'Like she knew you were on your way, it's weird.'

'That's because she probably did, I bumped into her in the Blacksmith' Ben said finally taking a sip of the warm coffee.

'Oh, did you talk to her or?'

'I bumped into her accidentally after I bought some Vodka Red Bulls for me and my mate.' Jack finally pulled out his book and started to jot things down. 'And your friends' name?'

'Troy Melwood.'

'Do you believe she saw him or would go for him as well, I'll have-'

 'No chance, he was passed out and laid on a backrest more or less. Dead to the world. He'll be in no state to work tomorrow.' Ben took a huge swig of his Costa, ingulfing it all down. Ben was a little worried about his friend. Mainly because he knew he'd fuck something up on the job and Ben would probably get blamed for it by the suits.

'So, start from the moment you walked into the toilets. What happened?' Ben had Jack's full attention.

'I walked in for a piss, tried flicking the lights on but they were all busted. I heard something like a dripping sound, and I noticed the far sink was full of water and trickling onto the floor.' Jack had a look of confusion on his face and asked 'Why?'

'I'm getting there, anyway so I walked over and there was a pasty and a can of Pepsi on the sink. Left for me because that's what I originally wanted from the garage after I had a piss. I don't know how she knew that. She knew a lot of things.' Ben started to choke up and his eyes began to gather liquid.

'What things did she know Ben?'

'She knew I killed my sister.' He said. Jack looked mortified as he heard the unspeakable confession. 'Not like that, it was an accident. I rolled over one night I was looking after her and I-' Ben burst into tears and jack rushed over to offer a sympathetic hand. 'It's ok Ben, take your time.' Jack was in no rush and this man was traumatised.

'I crushed her and suffocated her to death. She was so young and small, I got found innocent but I'm guilty as hell Jack. I took her life, that makes me no better than that bitch who attacked me.' Croaked Ben. Pure grief slapped across his bruised face.

'Hey, you are not a killer Mate, it was an accident.' Jack grabbed him gently and hugged him. Letting him know he believed him. 'What else did she know?'

'She said she knew where my parents were. I haven't spoken to them for so long because of that night. She said she would tell me after I told her something.' Ben looked as if he was about to cry again.

'What did you have to tell her Ben?' Jack looked more nervous now. Would it be a minor thing like how much did he weigh, or would it put the whole case in a shitstorm.

'She wanted to know where my co-worker Mike Ashburn lived.'

'WHAT!' why?'

'She didn't say, but after I told her, she asked me to say hello to my sister and tried to kill me. First, she punched me square on in the eye and then stamped on my chest before breaking both my legs. Then she put my head in the sink and attempted to drown me.' Ben explained as he expressed anger on his forehead. Jack was writing at speed in his notebook. 'Then I swung back with my arm and managed to hit her in her nose I think, I fell to the ground and just before she left she broke my fucking finger.'

'That's when she left?' asked Jack.

'Yeah, and then I crawled to that toilet and pulled myself up. I wasn't laying on that floor, you saw the state of it.' Jack looked at his notes and questioned what he had written.

'So she attempted to kill you and then just left, leaving a witness to her identity?' Jack was puzzled.

'Apparently so Jack.' Ben wiped his left cheek and smiled at him. 'I'm just glad I'm still living.'

'Me too Ben, you've been more than helpful sir now get some rest.' Jack stood up. 'Just one other thing, what is Mike's address?'

'Stone Brooke House, Regent street Apartment 49. Is he in trouble?' He asked feeling bad for telling the tale once again.

'No, I'm just going to check he's ok, clearly this woman wants to see him. Get some rest Ben.' Said Jack. He had already concluded that Mike was at the centre of all this. This woman could be his mother and if she was the 'Snapper' then he was in great danger. Just as he was about to leave the room, Ben said 'When you catch her, make sure she never gets up again.'

CHAPTER TWENTY-FIVE:

Mike had the rope in his hands as he stood over James, hopefully for the last time he thought. This was his ticket to freedom. To start his new project of hunting his mother down. He had been thinking about strangling her to death whilst he got himself together in the garage. James was laid facing his dead wife crying. The child was still sound asleep upstairs, he was a good father after all. Mike felt a little guilty about the fact he was robbing that poor kid of two parents but, as a killer, you had to be selfish to survive.

'Stand up.' Mike demanded. 'I can drag you through or you can walk with dignity.'

'Oh aren't you a fucking saint giving me a choice, huh?' James was filled with remorse and guilt, looking at his dead wife. All the things he couldn't put right. The time he had stayed out until 3 AM and cheated on her, twice. The time he broke her pearl necklace and blamed it on his son. All the chances to put all that right. Gone. The waterfall began to fall down his face, dripping onto the wooden floor. He stood up with great difficulty but not without dignity. The knife still stuck in his ankle. Mike noticed it and started to question it. Why would the Snapper have a knife in his foot? Because his wife defended herself and got a lucky shot in. He felt proud of his poor lie.

James hobbled along, gently. Blood now pouring out of the wound as the bone moved. His face was scrunched up in agony as he shuffled along. 'Where you want me?' Mike was shocked at how he had just accepted his fate. Willing to die without a fight. 'I do this, you do not touch my fucking son.'

James had fire behind his eyes. Mike nodded. A father's love burned bright in this one after all.

'I promise James.' Mike said as he met his stare. James nodded back, trusting a serial killer not to kill his son wasn't the plan of this evening. But at least Jake would hopefully live a full life. Mike gripped the rope even tighter. Feeling anxious as James hobbled on, he ran to the door and checked it was locked which it was. He then darted up the stairs and began to tie the rope around the banister. He couldn't wait for the Snapper to be off the earth. James made it to the bottom of the stairs, leaving a trail of blood. He looked at Mike, tying his fate around his bannister. James fell on the floor and rolled over, groaning in pain and taking the handle of the knife in his palm. If he was going to overpower him, it was now. Mike finished the knot and made his way down to him. To offer him a hand up. The least he could do if this man was going to take the blame. As he reached the bottom step and began to lower his body down to help him up, James ripped the knife out and swung it across Mikes chest. Catching him on right of his rib cage. Mike felt fire caress through his body. Like a thousand wasps stinging the inside of his muscles. He instinctively put his arm over the wound to stop the bleeding and kicked James as hard as his size 10 could be flung. James's eye socket popped open like a kinder surprise egg, spewing blood over his shoe. 'Fucking great.' Mike whispered as he collapsed over James's unconscious body. He knew he couldn't leave any blood behind. I was never here. He had to fix himself, now. The adrenaline gave him the strength to lift himself and more or less ran into the kitchen. He got a clean dish towel off the handle of the oven and ran it under the cold tap. He then got the Sellotape from the living room which was used to tie the 'Snapper' up. He taped the wet towel to his wound and whalah. Good as new. He had to do this now and do it quick.

He walked at a steady pace into the hallway and grabbed the knotted end of the rope. He slid it over James's almost dead body. Caressing his neck as the rope sat loosely on his Adam's apple. Mike's vision became a little blurred as the pressure went to his head. He struggled up the stairs and reached the point where the rope was tied. 'Now for the easy part.'

He pulled with all his might and James began to move along the floor, slowly but surely, he was up the first two steps. Mike could feel his t-shirt becoming wet. He had the cold faint feeling. His breathing began to deepen and become more rapid. He carried on pulling and James was up to the halfway point. Mike was relying on the pain to see him through. He turned the pain to anger and pulled as hard as he could. Trying to be as quiet as possible not to wake Jake. As he promised this poor soul, he wouldn't touch him. He was two steps off and Mike reached down and grabbed him by the shirt as well as having the rope in his right hand. He pulled with all his might and was transported back to the time he had a tug of war at Scout Dike.

He was up. James rested lifelessly on the floor. His lips twitched as he became to come back around. Mike's side was split open, deep. James really did a number on him. But it would be Mike who had the last laugh. He sat James up against the bannister and once again put pressure on his ribs. He couldn't help but feel sorry for James. He didn't deserve any of this, but there was no way he was going to prison. 'Fuck that.'

Mike bent down and grabbed him by the waist. Bear hugging him, he locked his fingers on the over side and began to lift. It took Mike two attempts to get James on the bannister. Perched like a sitting statue. Even with an open wound, he was still strong. But now he did feel faint. This was it. Time was up for the 'Snapper.' In a single push from Mike's right hand, James had committed suicide. He had murdered 5 women, one of whom was his wife. He had felt so guilty about it all he did the world a favour and hung himself in his own home. His wife got a lucky shot in which Mike would add to the note when he got downstairs. James's body hung swaying from side to side. Mike was surprised how quiet the ordeal was, he was shocked the kid was still asleep. He shuffled downstairs and took a glance at James's corpse. He felt proud. He entered the kitchen, and everything became a blur. He fell to the ground headfirst. Surely Jake heard that.

CHAPTER TWENTY-SIX:

Emily woke up in the arms of Amy. She didn't feel guilt. She felt happy. For the first time in a long time, she felt whole again. She would be lying if she said she didn't have any feelings for Amy. She thought she didn't. She thought she was better off alone, but how wrong she was. She cuddled up to her tighter. Enjoying the quiet night feeling protected from anything the world threw at her. The rain had subsided for the first time in a while. She craved Amy's presence. For the first time since she could remember, she didn't feel the need to sniff any coke. She just wanted love.

A loud knock came from the hallway and woke Amy up instantly. 'That mine?' she asked still half asleep.

'No, across the hall.' She answered her question and followed with a peck on the lips. Another loud knock. Amy let out a louder yawn and a groan like a spoilt child. 'I hope they fuck off soon.' She rolled over letting Em free of her clutches. Another loud knock.

'Fuck this, one sec-'Emily rose out of bed and checked the clock on the wall. 11:57 PM. The fact it was late made her mad. She rushed to Amy's door and swung it open with some force. Before her stood detective Jack Brown.

'Hey, asshole. Any idea what time it is?' She asked in a stern voice. The man was dressed in a shirt and tie and casual jeans. Almost dressed like he hasn't changed in a couple of days.

Like he'd been living sofa to sofa. Hair messy and heavy bags hanging from his eyes. He looked ill.

'I do, I'm looking for Mike Ashburn.' Stated Jack.

'Who's asking?' Her arms folded, genuinely concerned. Mike never had any visitors.

'DCI Jack Brown, South Yorkshire.' He held out his badge and to his surprise, she apologised for her language.

'He not Home yet?' She was concerned now. 'He never stops out this late. Must have a date.' Jack struck her with the evillest look his face could conjure up.

'you know him?'

'Kind of, see him now and again.' She lied. She had learned overtime to keep her trap shut when talking to the pigs.

'What do you mean, kind of?' His eyes still glued to her.

'Like, I see him in the hall once in a while, why?' She lied once again. 'He done something wrong?' Jack looked back at the door and decided he wasn't in. 3 knocks and he hadn't heard a peep from inside the flat. Only the bark of a dog.

'If you see him, tell him to ring me ASAP.' He slid one of his cards under the door and walked back to the exit. Staring at Emily as he walked past her. I've seen her somewhere before he thought. But where?

He opened the door and entered the stale breeze of the Town centre. Stale kebab meat and loud shouting still echoed through the town. The party still in full swing. He had two choices. Go home and get some rest or stay here and wait for Mike to show up. He decided to go home and get some rest, Mike could wait until the morning. He headed to his poorly parked car and drove home. Speeding all the way there.

'Who was it?' Amy laid on Emily's side fully awake now. Waiting for her to re-enter her bedroom.

'A detective, looking for Mike.' Said Emily. She entered the bedroom just as another loud knock came from the hallway. 'For god sake!' She spun around and headed for the front door again and as before, swung it open with some force. 'Isn't it obvious that he- 'Emily froze. 'Shit.'

'So, this is where you are.' Liz stood outside Mike's with the facial expression of a woman who had just had her heart shattered into a thousand pieces. 'How long?'

'How long what?' Asked Emily, even though she knew what she meant. Liz's eyes began to water. 'How long have you two been fucking?' Liz's usual soft voice was that of a demon-like creature. Croaky and razor-like.

'Look, we're not fucking…' Emily trailed off. 'This was the first time…' she didn't know how to tell her the truth. 'I don't want to be with you anymore.' She said, surprising herself. She normally ran from the truth and bad situations, this was a positive step forward for her.

'WHAT! WHY?' Liz's torn apart voice shouted. Loud enough for the whole floor to wake up. The end Flat door creaked open and a man in his late 30's stepped out. Looked them both up and down and went back inside.

'Because...' Emily couldn't speak the truth, she didn't have the balls to tell her how annoying she was and how she smothered her. She felt so smothered that she couldn't breathe.

'Because I love her.' She said. It was kind of true, but she was still in denial at the fact. Why else would she spend the night?

'You're a cunt.' Hissed Liz. 'Fuck you!' she power-walked down the hall and out of Emily's life. Emily hung in the hallway calming herself down. Still in disbelief at what she had just done. She was free, she felt revitalised. All she wanted right now was to be with Amy and drift off to sleep. As she re-entered Amy's, she checked the clock once again and it was 12:01 AM. One thought hung in her mind like a pendulum. Where the fuck is Mike?

Liz exited Stone Brooke house a single woman. It was late but she didn't care, she had already made her mind up about phoning in sick, again. No matter how hard she tried she always felt like she wasn't good enough. All she had done for Emily was show her love and support. So why had she fallen for someone else? Her head was spinning with all kinds of conclusions. But one feeling hung heavier than the others. Revenge.' I want that bitch to feel how I feel. To have her heart ripped out and stamped on for no apparent reason.' She wiped away her tears and headed home. Not noticing the stranger across the street who was following her route. She walked through the centre feeling like an empty bag, she reached Dog Lane. A long alleyway which led on to the main road where she had parked her car. The best place to park if you don't want the drunks to vomit all over your vehicle. She looked down the long dark path. No streetlights, no cameras.

Just concrete and probably homeless people. She took a deep breath and set off walking. 'I don't even care if anything happens, what do I have to fucking lose anyway.' She stopped dead on the spot as she heard footsteps from behind her. The hooded stranger lunged her stomach with a long, stainless steel blade from behind her and replied, 'Your life.' Liz felt cold all of a sudden. Feint and weak.

She fell to her knees with the black handle still sticking out of her and glanced at her attacker. A wrinkly woman stood towering over her dying body and smirked.

'She didn't love you did she Liz. Don't worry I'll make her pay for your death.' Liz fell back onto the damp concrete.

'D-don't you t-touch her.' She quivered as she laid there beginning to fade away. The stranger stood over her, menacingly.

'What you going to do about it, you'll be dead.' She grasped the handle of the blade and yanked it out. Spraying blood all over Liz's young face. She began to shake, blood spewed out of her open wound. She stared at the night sky as the light in her eye died out. Like an old star. She laid there and eventually bled out. The stranger wiped the blade with her sleeve, using the crease in her arm as she bent her elbow upward. It was clean but her clothes were not. She needed to disappear, fast. She could finally go home now she had satisfied her sick desire. She smiled as she looked at Liz. 'Shame, she was a pretty girl.' She turned around and headed out of the shadows.

CHAPTER TWENTY-SEVEN:

Mike opened his eyes, to his surprise he was still at the fifth victims' home. He tried to stand but was met with great pain in his torso, nagging his ribs like a child wanting candy. His head was pounding as he realised he wasn't alone. He was standing just to his right, looking down on him like an animal wanting to be put out of its misery. 'You've fucked up Mike.'

'How have I?' He questioned, struggling to speak. Looking around as if the answer would be so easy to pinpoint.

'Well, you're not exactly in good shape are you?' His conscience was right. This was the first time anyone had taken him on, and by god, they had done a number on him. His blood had started to pool around him, soaking through the old wash towel. Mike struggled to sit up, but he did it with great difficulty. Blood dripped from his left arm as he rubbed his tired eyes. 'You're going to get caught, how the hell are you going to make it back to your apartment?'

Mike stared into the hallway and could just see the bottoms of James's feet, dangling. I forgot I managed to hang him he thought. His annoying manifestation of himself was right, he was annoying, but he was right. There was no way he could make it home in his condition, he needed medical attention.

'That's exactly what I need.' He said to himself. 'I need medical attention… because I was also attacked by the Snapper… when I heard him murdering his wife and ran in to help her.'

'Oh, Jesus. That is the dumbest fucking idea you have ever had, you crazy prick.' Said his conscience, now leaning on the worktop reading the suicide note.

'Who the fuck are you anyway?' asked Mike, rubbing his eyes once more. Seeing if he would still be there when he closed his eyes.

'I'm your conscience. Like all your deepest thoughts what you don't want to know about. Because they're real. You've suppressed me so long I've come to the surface. It's unhealthy. I know everything about you. Your kills, your so-called relationship with your mommy. I know all of it, Mike. Because I'm a part of that. You are mentally ill. That's the real reason you see me.'

'Huh, so you're like what my side-kick?' Mike coughed as he felt faint once again.

'SURE!, crazy twat. You think people are going to believe that bullshit note? Dude, I don't even believe it and I'm you.' He said tapping the note. Demonstrating there was no noise from his finger connecting with the solid wood.

'OH! You just reminded me about- '

'Adding more to it? Your thinking of the wrong action.'

'What?'

'Think about it, if you're going to play the victim, what would a victim do?' Mike looked puzzled. He'd never been a murder victim before, or an attempted murder victim for that matter. His sidekick was right, he needed to be a victim to be able to survive this. So many things had gone wrong already.

'If I was a victim I'd probably want to crawl out on to the street. To get help.'

'Bingo, that's the one. Now you're going to need two things.' Mike laid on the floor facing the front door and began to crawl slowly.

'W-What's that T-Then?' He struggled for breath as he spoke.

'One, make your bullshit believable and two you're going to want to make the kid believe his daddy was the killer and not you.' Just as Mike exited the kitchen and got next to the photo he smashed (Luckily none of his blood had stained the glass as he punched it) a little voice from landing said 'Daddy, I want some water.' Mike's heart dropped into his stomach like an elevator cable had just snapped. Two options ran through his troubled mind. Play dead or scream for help. 'What would a victim do?' he whispered to himself. With the child's footsteps getting closer Mike decided to beat him to the scream, but he was too late. Jake let out a scream so loud it surely damaged Mike's eardrums. Well, so he thought. The child had just been robbed of his innocence.

'CALL THE POLICE!' he shouted as loud as he could. The child ran back into his room, sobbing and screaming. Mike felt utter guilt as he laid in the Hallway, with no reply as to what was happening. He would have to wait until he woke up again to find out how this ordeal concluded.

CHAPTER TWENTY-EIGHT:

Ben stared at the wall which seemed to get closer every time he took his eyes off it. Closing in on him, slowly but surely. He began to feel uneasy. Lightheaded and a little sick. The feeling of being closed in and possibly suffocated was unbearable. A tear slipped from his duct as he thought of waking up that night to his mum and dad screaming in pure terror at him. The words 'WHAT HAVE YOU DONE!' rang in his head since he was 14. Always ringing, like a phone salesman or the bell of a hotel lobby. Always ringing. It felt later than it was. Ben was sure it was past 2 AM but it was

1:17 AM. He was restless, images of his attacker tormented his troubled mind. A little TV was needed, his favourite past time, to pass a little time. He pulled the TV which hung from the roof. Set it hanging a couple of inches from his fat face and tried to shuffle himself into a little more comfort but was greeted by the sharp shooting pain of his broken legs. A small groan was masked by his closed mouth, making sure he didn't wake anyone else.

He pulled the earphones off the screen he paid £7.99 for and pressed the small power button. The silent screen illuminated 001 for BBC 1. This hour was rerunning news from the previous day, Ben had already seen it all. But he hadn't seen the latest breaking news on the bottom right-hand side. In a box half the size of the screen read. BREAKING NEWS: THE SNAPPER FOUND DEAD AT HIS HOME IN BARNSLEY.

'His?...so who was that woman who tried to kill me?'

Jack swung his car into the driveway just behind the 'twat mobile.' He flung his door open with some force. He was the first on the scene. The call had come from a child claiming his mommy and daddy were dead at home with a bleeding man. Jack's phone had buzzed from dispatch, just 5 minutes after he managed to drift off. He answered and shot out of bed to the news that this man was James Watson. He knew him. Decent enough friends from school often kept in touch through the basic social media. A message now and again to see how each other was doing. Sometimes even went to the Blacksmith for a catch-up, leading on to the Swivel bar for some poor attempts of pulling a bird. Jake his son said his daddy had left a note saying he was the Snapper. But Jack felt he knew James enough to know he wasn't a serial killer. Or did he?

He more or less put the front door through he shoved it that hard on his entrance. What his eyes displayed for him to see was beyond shocking. A man lying on the floor face down with a trail of blood scratched into the wood floor behind him, a woman, Loraine Watson who he had met the odd time, laying lifeless with bruising around her thin neck. His friend James, hanging like a leaf in the summer breeze off a branch. Jack was fully focused on his old friend. His eyes closed. Blood still dripping off his ankle. He guessed the wound was done by the knife which laid by the side of his dead wife. He didn't even notice the frightened child perched on the steps, head in between his legs. 'Hey, Hey, it's okay.' Jack rushed towards the small boy. 'What's your name pal?' Asked the shocked detective.

'Jake.' He sniffled with tears.

'Come with me, my little dude.' Said Jack thinking the word dude would make him feel cool. But he didn't feel cool, he wouldn't feel anything but sadness and loss for the remainder of his life. Jack chaperoned him outside and wait for his team to arrive. 'Let's get you outside Huh?'

He waited five minutes before the crew arrived. Back up police officers began to secure the area and a few over detectives began to knock on some door for witnesses. The forensics got busy and began to assess the situation. The ambulance crew tended to the two bodies on the floor. The woman was put in a body bag, but the male was put on a stretcher. 'He's alive let's get him to hozi.' One Paramedic said to the other and they did exactly that. Jack headed back inside but to his surprise was called back by Sargent Scott Dickinson. 'JACK!' The air seemed to shake as his words traveled through the particles. Jack almost sighed, he wanted to do some detective work instead of filling his boss in on the situation.

'Fill me in, the situation.' Said Sargent Dickinson. His moustache hiding the expression his mouth was displaying. Jack wasn't in the mood and he knew he could tell a lie from the truth, so he just came right out with it. Exactly what they were dealing with.

'We've got 3 bodies. One hanging by a noose, a dead woman and as far as I'm aware one is alive on the way to the Northern General. That little boy over there is the son of the one hanging and the female. Apparently, there is a note which the 'Snapper' has left.' He finally took a breath.

'You say apparently a lot Jack.'

'That's because I just went in and got the boy out- '

'Wait. You mean the Snapper is dead, and hanging by that noose in there?'

'Uh.. I'm not sure without- '

'Well get in there and find out, will you.' The Sargent wasn't happy. The voice he used was firm. Like an Army General. Jack turned around and rushed inside, out of his way.

He walked through the hallway and said. 'Bag anything which could be used as evidence boys. That picture, need that.' He pointed to the broken photograph. 'Cut him down.' He demanded

'But, sir we haven't taken our samples of the rope or- '

'Did I fucking stutter? I said cut him down. NOW! You can get your samples while he's down can't you?' He carried on walking through the house, checking for any more evidence. 'Bag the knife' he carried on into the living room and saw two people brushing for prints. 'Bag that' he said pointing to the Sellotape. He finally stood still and took it all in.

James Watson, the man who in the end had murdered five women in four months, destroying his family in the process. 'Dumb basted.' He said under his breath as he stared at the proud family portrait which hung behind the sofa. He heard the tap his bosses' shoes made on a wooden floor. 'Couldn't wait for me to do my job, eh?' He said.

'You know me, always been eager.' Dickinson said. Then joining him looking at the portrait. 'What do you think?'

'Not sure, let me read the note and I'll get back to you.' He spun on the spot and headed to the kitchen. He looked around the messy kitchen. Blood and a drenched towel stained the floor. He hated blood but it came with the job. He spotted the note, with ease and read it. Not touching it or damaging the prints on it (If there were any.) He stepped back in disbelief and spotted a wallet perched neatly on the table. He opened it and was surprised by the picture.

'Well, what we got?' The sergeants' question hung in the air like a horrible smell.'

'I think James is being set up. That's not his handwriting. I'm going to go to the hospital to get some answers off Mike Ashburn.'

'Who the fuck is Mike Ashburn?' Asked Scott.

'The guy who lied about Lauren's phone call. The guy who is being hunted by the woman who attacked Ben Hanson in the Royston. The guy who keeps popping up on my radar.'

'So the woman who attacked Mr Hanson isn't the Snapper then?' And to his Sergeants' plea to stay and chat, he was already getting back in his car. Jack sped off in the night sky, not seeing the stranger who lurked in the street. Unnoticed, as always.

CHAPTER TWENTY-NINE:

Mike's eyes flickered open. He wasn't at the dream house anymore. He was in a clean place. Which stunk to high heaven of disinfectant. He was laid on his back facing the roof. His head was still pounding (as always it seemed) and his chest was burning a lot more now. He grunted and groaned as the tubes which were sticking out of him were clacking against the heart monitor.

'You've lost a lot of blood sir, just take it easy.' A pretty looking nurse said. 'You're lucky you got out of there alive.' She looked at him as if he was a hero. She checked his chart and told him about his wound on his chest. It would heal nicely and once again he was lucky the maniac only sliced a couple of millimetres into him.

Just like that, he remembered. The lies, the mislead and playing the victim seemed to have worked. Worked a treat. 'Once we get you hydrated, and you've spoken to the police about what happened. You'll probably be out of here by dinner time tomorrow. Well, later today.'

'I thought you said I've lost a lot of blood?' questioned Mike.

'You did, but your all good now, we did the transfusion as soon as you arrived, sir.' Mike let worry set in like a welcomed guest. He didn't know what to tell the police, he would have to make up a believable story within the hour. This was the case of the Snapper which had zero leads. This he knew due to the lack of coverage by the media. But right now he just wanted to sleep.

'Thankyou nurse. I'm going to get some rest now.' She smiled and exited the room and out into the ward. Mike's eyes started to shut when he got a glance of him. His sidekick stood at the end of his bed with a huge smile on his face. 'You're fucked.'

'Jack Brown.' He said flashing his badge to the same receptionist as before.

'I know, you here for the slasher victim?'

'Snapper.' He replied. She clicked and clacked on her keyboard, itching her nose and altering her jam jar glasses again. 'Down the hall last door on the left, if he's asleep don't wake him. He's one of the lucky ones.' She stated.

'We'll see.' He left the desk and set off, almost power walking down the hallway. He reached the door and saw Mike in a room all on his own. He checked the corridors and saw no one in sight. He could see he had his eyes tight shut. His chest moving up and down, slowly. Almost struggling. 'I'll come back tomorrow.' He said to the unfortunate victim. He turned on his heels and headed home. He needed answers but waking him up to talk at this time would do none of them any good. Jack was tired, and Mike surely wouldn't be in a fit state to remains yet. He reached the elevator and pressed the ground floor. He exited the hospital and headed for his car. Jack couldn't get the image of James hanging by his neck in his own home. He decided to swing by the crime scene one more time just to check he hadn't missed anything, sleep could wait.

He pulled up behind the twat mobile again and switched his engine. He entered the bitter breeze and stared at the house. His team was still working the grounds but at least the Neighbours had lost interest. He turned around and faced the woodland are which surrounded them. Tall trees and bushy shrubbery concealed the street. Mike couldn't help but notice something blowing about on the floor. He bent down, crouching and was greeted by a cigarette butt. He picked it up, gently. 'Hey, Bob! Hand me a bag!' Bob rushed out of the house with an evidence bag, he was in a split second.

'What you found boss?' He asked, shivering.

'Tab end.' Replied Jack still staring at it in the plastic bag.

'Oh, why's it evidence? It could have blown in from anywhere.' Bob said. Sounding full of confidence.

'Doubt it. Look around at the property. There's nothing but woods other than the house next door, and I don't think they would flick tab ends into the Watsons.'

'So, who's could it be?'

'We can rule out the Watsons. James had never smoked in his life.'

'What about the wife, Loraine?'

'Run it for DNA with the rest and we'll see what we have.'

CHAPTER THIRTY:

Ryan reached the end of smith's row before he turned the corner which led to meadow lane. Goldthorpe wasn't the best place but some areas were quiet enough. Ryan's parents did mind him still living at home. After all, he was only twenty-one years old, and he wasn't ready for the world as his mother says. She also says she's glad he still lives at home since there was a serial killer on the loose in Barnsley. He walked in the rain, embracing it. Not knowing he was being followed. He hummed away to his music, all happy because he had just finished his shift. 'Hello, Ryan.' A voice said unaware he had earphones in. She reached out and caressed his skinny shoulder. He jumped and let out a little yelp as he spun around. 'JESUS! What do you want?' He asked as he pulled his earphones out.

'A word.' She turned around and set off walking, Ryan checked none of his neighbours were peeking and followed her.

'Well, what the fuck happened?' She pulled down her hood to reveal her greyish blonde hair. The light from the lamppost above her made her wrinkles stand out.

'I gave the USB drive Sal, I had to.'

'You didn't! you could have kept your mouth shut and he would have believed the footage was destroyed thanks to me smashing it all up.' Her face had turned sour. 'I thought you wanted to help me? Revenge for your sister?'

'I do! I just…. He guilt-tripped me.' Murmured Ryan embarrassed.

'Listen to me. Betray me like that again and you'll be joining her.' Ryan was shocked at her statement but was understandable. He would have reacted the same way.

'I thought you were going home after you killed Ben?'

'I was, but I didn't end up killing him. I thought I'd let him live after all he did what I asked in the end.'

'So you felt bad?'

'I never feel bad. I killed a bitch in the town. Stabbed her. I've got one more stop before I go home.' Ryan looked confused at the fact she couldn't kill Ben but could kill a random woman in the town.

'I need to go put a dog down.' Ryan's face dropped. Realising just how evil she was. 'We're going to make him suffer for killing Lauren, mark my words.' She set off walking without uttering a word goodbye to him. Ryan stood for a minute, just taking all of it in. The whole killing thing didn't sit right with him, that's why he told Jack about the USB drive. Because it was the right thing to do. He took a deep breath and watched her disappear down a narrow genel. He turned around and set off back home. He didn't feel bad that the man who had killed his sister was about to lose his dog, but he did feel bad for the innocent pooch.

That following morning Mike opened his eyes to the same room he was in last night. The same nurse was at the opposite end of the room reading his chart. He tried to sit up, but he was sore. Sorer than last night. He needed some painkillers. 'Nurse…Nurse can I-'

'On the way.' She replied and exited the room. She hurried straight back with two pills and a glass of water. 'Take it easy, your wound will be a little sore still.' Mike looked down at his chest to see his blood had stained his dressing. 'Could I use a phone please, I need to make arrangements for my dog. He's been alone all this time.'

'Sure I'll let you use my mobile.' The Nurse once again left the room. Mike was worried about his best bud. He hoped he hadn't pissed everywhere. But then again it could be worse. He could be in custody and never see his best friend. The nurse tossed him her phone and gave him a cheeky wink. He dialed a number he knew well, the only number he ever really used. He pushed the green button and waited for the line to become active.

'Hello?' Answered Emily in a tired voice. Still tired from the wild night she had.

'Em, it's Mike I need another favour if you could please. Another £80 in it for you.' He knew she never turned down easy money.

'I'm listening…' She said now sitting up in bed.

'Can you go take care of Marley please, I'm in hospital but I should be out for dinner, all being well.'

'Hospital? You alright?' She asked. Amy woke up to worrying news and leaned her ear against the phone to try and listen in.

'I'm okay, long story can you do it? Please.' He knew she wouldn't be able to say no.

'Leave it with me. Oh! Another thing, there was a detective at your flat last night.' Emily heard Mike let a deep sigh. A sigh of worry.

'Why?'

'He didn't say, he came late though. Looked like he had just run a fucking marathon.'

'And you were still in my building why….' He teased. He knew exactly why.

'Long story, get well soon Mike.' The line went dead. He had noticed the nurse hanging on the door frame waiting for her phone about mid-way through the conversation. 'Thank you.' He said holding the phone in mid-air. She took it from him and walked once again out of the room. Mike tried to adjust himself and this time there wasn't any pain.

'Mike Ashburn.' Mike knew that voice. He had heard a yesterday while he was interviewed about Lauren. He turned his head and his memory didn't let him down. 'Jack Brown, what can I do for you?'

CHAPTER THIRTY-ONE:

Jack walked into the room and held out a hand to the chair at the side of his bed. 'May I?'

'Of course.' He had nothing to hide, after all, he was a victim. The gash which led a path across his chest reminded him of that. Jack pulled the chair away from his bed and sat comfortably not even a foot away from him. Jack ran his beady eyes across Mike, examining everything. His drip was on the dressing on his chest. His bare legs. Jack wrote it all down in his trusty book. Holding it tight like it would jump out of his hands at any moment. Mike didn't want to say anything first, he acted as he was in discomfort, which he was but not enough to cause a fuss. He tried his best to look uncomfortable. Maybe the DCI would go easy on him. Mike looked up at the ceiling, all he could see was James hanging. Swaying gently in the house of horror. 'What happened Mike?' Asked Jack. Staring at him, supporting an expression as if Mike had done something wrong.

'He tried to kill her.' He whispered as quiet as he could, but Jack heard it.

'No, I mean what happened. How did you get that?' He pointed his ballpoint to his dressing. 'Start from the beginning, no rush.' Jack brought his left leg over his right one a fidgeted until he was comfortable. Mike took a deep breath and a little gulp before he began.

'It was around eight-thirty, I was at home, I'd just had my tea…' he itched his left eye. 'I was bored, so I thought I'd go for a walk. I live around ten minutes away from Smithies Lane. I was going to walk down there and then cut back through the Gypsy field. A decent half an hour walk.'

'Any reason you chose Smithies lane?' Jack said not looking up from his book to see Mike's face had begun to turn a little red.

'Warm?' He asked.

'A little, I chose Smithies Lane because of its beautiful surroundings.'

'You mean the woods.' Said Jack jotting the word WOODS in capital letters on the white paper. He looked up and stuck his eyes on Mike, waiting for his response. But he was still. Almost frozen.

'Yes, the woods. You see when I was growing up me and my father used to go fishing on the Dearne, it just reminds me of those times. All the trees, the leaves, especially the earthy smell.' Mike looked at him, then quickly glanced at the window at the far end of his room. The rain had started once again. Leaving Mike feeling a little safer than before.

'Continue.' Spat Jack.

'Anyway, as I was walking just over the hump (A big rise on Smithies lane, almost a hill) I noticed a car fly past me, it was traveling at some speed. It had offensive words and images spray-painted on the bodywork. Anyway, it turned out to be his as I saw it screech onto his driveway. I thought nothing of it, a man is allowed to do as he pleases on his property. But when he got out… there was something off with him.'

'Off?' Jack's eyebrows raised as he halted his scribbling.

'Yeah, like he didn't even close his car door (Mike had noticed as he went into the garage and could see the door hanging open) and he sprinted inside. Not ran, like sprinted like he was going for gold, he slammed his door shut, loud enough for me to hear it up on the hump.' Mike finished and reached for the water jug on his side. His right arm started to pull his stitches open as he reached and let out a huge yelp. Like a dog who had just had its paw stood on. To his surprise, Jack poured a glass and served him it with a trusty smile.

'Thank you.' Said Mike. Jack sat back down and open up his book again.

'So you saw him sprint into the house, then what?' Jack was eager. No time for hanging around he wanted the scoop. Now

'I carried on walking and lit up a smoke. As I said I thought nothing of it until I reached outside the property and that's when I heard a woman scream. I tossed my smoke in their garden and rushed up to their door.'

'That explains the fag butt I found under his wheel. James didn't smoke. I knew him personally.' Jack proudly admitted.

'Yeah, well it was mine, anyway I looked through one of the panels of glass and saw him with his hands on her throat, so I opened the door and luckily it was unlocked.' How was it lucky? She still died you muppet. All you did was get yourself involved in all this thought Jack.

'I startled him, he averted his attention to me just long enough for her stab his ankle.'

'where was the knife?'

'It was on the floor. As I walked in he had both hands on her throat…'

'Hmmm'

'He looked at me and she got both her arms under his and broke free. He looked back at her, but she was quick and stuck the knife in his right ankle, I believe it was the right.' Mike finally finished, looking at the detective jotting his every word into his book. Jack finished and looked up.

'So she managed to get one over him, then what?'

'Then I charged. I acted on impulse and rushed at him, he ripped out the knife as I ran and by the time I arrived at the end where he was, it was waiting for. As I ran he swung but I slowed my self and leaned back if you get me? I believe that's why the knife didn't go deep.'

'But you did lose a lot of blood…tell me, after you got sliced what happened after that.' Asked Jack.

'I…it's a blur. I think I hit something and busted my nose as I fell. I grabbed a tea towel off the oven and applied pressure to the wound, then I woke up here.'

'That's all you can remember?' Jack had halted his scribbling once again and gazed directly into his eyes.

'Yes.' Mike lied. Jack unfolded his legs. closed his book and leaned forward. 'Mike, we found your wallet on his kitchen counter. Just your wallet and nothing else other than the note. Like he took it out of your pocket.'

'He must have because I defiantly had it. I planned to pick up a pizza from the town.' Mike said, still sounding a little uneasy. Jack leaned back in the chair and prepared himself. 'Can I ask you something. Off the record?'

'I guess.' Mike was nervous now, what could it be that it had to be off the record. Did he know the truth? Had he worked it out already?

'What's your relationship like with your mother?'

'My mother?'

'Yeah. Do you see her at all?' asked The DCI. Mike looked puzzled but decided to answer truthfully. Well almost.

'Honestly, no, we aren't on speaking terms.' Stated Mike.

'Well, I believe she's back in town Mike. I know she hasn't been seen in a while but last night I got a call to the Jet garage.' Mike's eyes widened. How could she be back? She had nothing left in Barnsley, so he thought. 'There had been an attempted Murder on your colleague Ben Hanson.'

Mike sat up as best he could, in disbelief. Had Ben nearly been killed just because he knew Mike? 'MY GOD! Is he ok?' Mike shouted in genuine shock.

'He's recovering, but he's in a bad way. Anyway, his attacker wanted your address, Mike.'

'My address? The fuck?' Mike scoffed. He didn't know what to think. He rubbed his hand through his thick as Jack stood up.

'I have a photograph from the CCTV footage. All I need is an ID that it's your mother Mike and then I know who I'm looking for.' Jack gazed at him once again with a look that asked, please tell me it's her. He pulled the A4 sheet of paper from his inside pocket and held it out between his index finger and thumb. Mike glanced at it and that was all he needed. There she was. Sally Ashburn in all of her glory. Her miserable existence had led right to her death. When Mike bumped into her next, she was dead. But he couldn't kill her if she was banged up.

'No, that's not my mum.' He said, calmly.

'You're sure Mike?' Jack stared with his head cocked to the left. Like a puppy when it hears a new sound.

'I haven't seen her in ages Jack, she will have changed but I can tell you that is not her. One hundred percent.' Jack let his arm fall and slap his side, still holding the photo. Mike gulped as he had saved her from his cuffs but not from his hands. A set of bongo drums began to echo from Jacks pocket, and he pulled out his phone. 'I have to go but I think I have everything I need. I'll be in touch.' And before Mike could reply, he was gone. Relief washed over Mike like the rain on Smithies lane did last night. Had he done it? Fooled the DCI in charge. Fooled him of his true identity and his mother's. He felt great like he was on top of the world once again, but deep down he had a feeling something bad was going to happen.

CHAPTER THIRTY-TWO:

'Jack Brown.' He answered. 'Ok.' He jumped in his car he had parked not too far away from the front doors and headed to the latest crime scene. Just five minutes later, he had arrived. He pulled up in the Underground carpark. The Underground was a lot like the Swivel, popular at night and infused with addicts, but dead through the day. Jack exited his car with nothing more than his phone in his hand. He power-walked through the barrier and blockade of officers, flashing his badge of entry. He arrived to find some of the forensics team hard at work, some having a quick fag break. He looked down at the girl's body. A clean wound in the stomach area and a pool of blood told the whole story.

'Jack!' shouted a rather familiar voice. 'Sarge.' He replied. The main man looked a little happier than usual which was weird since there was a serial killer running around the streets, doing whatever he or she wanted. Everyone believed James Watson was the killer, but not Jack. He didn't know what to believe.

'Well, was it her?' He asked.

'No, apparently he is one hundred percent sure it's not his mum but…'

'But what?' Jack replied with a shrug of the shoulders. 'I just feel like we shouldn't rule it out, I mean why else would this nutter want to know where Mike lives? He isn't exactly a somebody. You know what I mean?' Jack said, holding his arms out as he had been talking with them.

'I do. Okay well keep your eyes open for her- 'his phone cut his sentence short. He answered and agreed and disagreed before saying 'We need to go to the station.' The sarge headed to his car and Jack followed.

They had been in Sargent Dickinson's office five minutes with a coffee each before Jack uttered 'what are we doing here?'

'Relax, I know you feel bad for leaving the scene, but this is important Jack.' said the sarge in that famous stern tone. Jack sat still and waited for whatever it was they were waiting for. A knock on the panel of glass echoed and made them both jump. 'Come in!' shouted Dickinson. A tall lean man entered with an A4 file. His hair neatly pressed, and his suit was tailored to his slim shape. 'Gentlemen.' Said the man. Both officers rose from there the seats.

'Jack this is Tony ridings, a friend of mine and a man who knows how to get things.'

'Pleasure.' Replied Jack shaking his hand, firmly. They all sat after been offered a seat by the boss. His office was fairly sized but very plain. He didn't mind, he thought photos and wall hangings were distractions.

'Guys, I won't waste your time as I know your busy with this 'Snapper' case. But I do have what you wanted.'

'And what did we want?' asked Jack as soon as he realised he was left in the dark. Again.

'Pictures, evidence of that woman who followed Mr Hanson to Royston. Enough of the stuff to get a manhunt on the way.' The boss looked proud as he finished spitting as he spoke. Jack picked up the file from the white table and opened it to see CCTV frames of stills. A picture of Ben standing in a queue with her just close enough to be in the shot. Another one of her walking past the big stone which said ROYSTON as you entered the village. And finally, one of her walking past the bus station an hour after Ben had been attacked. Jack ran his hand through his greasy hair. It reminded him he had to shower today.

'If the time of death of the latest body is somewhat just before or after that time.' He said tapping the bottom corner where the time had been printed. 'We may have caught her just before or after the murder.'

'The question is though, is it the same woman from your photograph?' Asked Dickinson. Jack pulled out the creased up piece of paper and threw it on the table. It glided and landed at the side of the first picture. 'Jackpot.' Smiled Jack.

'Get a team and get the feelers out. I want this woman found and brought in for questioning.' The sarge demanded.

'On it.' Jack replied as he rushed out of the office. Finally, finally a lead! He thought as he rushed down the stairs. His legs couldn't carry him fast enough.

CHAPTER THIRTY-THREE:

Mike had been discharged with a couple of stitches and a speech about how he was a lucky man. The news was all over the latest story that James was the 'Snapper' and had taken his wife with himself, and Mike didn't feel one little bit guilty about it. After all, he was the victim that night. He entered Stone Brooke and headed for his flat.

'So, you got away with it. Got to say I'm pretty impressed. So what's the plan now that your free? Going to kill your mommy then play the victim again?' His conscience stood in front of the door he had just swung open. Looking calm.

'No. I'm going to show her what she needs to know.'

'And what's that huh? That you're a serial killer?'

'No, that you can't just abuse people and get away with it.' He turned his back and began to take a step.

'Exactly. Everything has a price, Mike. You're the biggest storm this town has ever seen. What price will you pay?' He turned around to see he had gone. He did give Mike something to think about, he was right. His mother had treated him badly and the price she was going to pay was her life. So what would be his?

He reached his door and slid his key in the lock and turned the mechanism freeing the door open. 'Marls, I'm home buddy!' he shouted as he steadily entered. He took a look back out in the hallway and saw himself standing at the end. Starting to freak me out a little he thought as he closed the wood door. 'Buddy?' he walked through the hallway passed the bedroom and bathroom and into the kitchen. His eyes widened and tears filled his eyes. 'No…..oh god no…..' He fell to his knees and began to cry. His head began to turn red and veins popped out of his neck. Marley laid on his sofa, his white fur stained red from the wound slashed across Emily's neck. She sat upright on the floor with his wallet on her lap with a note which read 'Your welcome.' '

'No! No! No!' he carried on screaming at the top of his lungs. His throat became dry as he grieved. He gathered himself and looked at the pair of them. Mike didn't know a lot, but he did know one thing. His mother was going to pay. First his father, now his dog and his beloved friend. To be honest his only true friend. His phone rang loud, but he didn't flinch. The number was withheld. He swiped the green icon as fast as he could.

'Yes?' He said as calmly as he could. Trying not to let slip he had tears in his eyes.

'Did you find your wallet son?' Sally teased, followed by a little chuckle.

'I found it ok. Let's hope the police can find your body that easy.' He pushed the red icon and threw his phone at the wall. Hard. Shattering it into a thousand pieces. Mike had one thing on his mind. not to call the police, not to bury his beloved pet, but to find Sally Ashburn and make her pay. She made it personal, so he would make it painful. Very painful.

Printed in Poland
by Amazon Fulfillment
Poland Sp. z o.o., Wrocław